The Teenager's Book of Life

DEDICATION

This book is dedicated to Jerome, Jesse, Oisín, Méabh, Sadbh, Isabelle, Ailbhe, Peter, Iarla, Reuben, Finn, Clara, Artemis, Jude, Taylor, Saoirse, Griffin, Michael, Julia, Ava and Sophie Slein. May you all have great adventures and always remember there is no one else like you in the world and we like you just the way you are.

A portion of the proceeds from the sale of this book will go to the Soar Foundation, which does life-changing work developing character and potential in teenagers.

TONY GRIFFIN

The Teenager's Book of Life

ILLUSTRATIONS BY **HAZEL BREEN**

SoulPlace Publishing

First published in 2020 by
SoulPlace Publishing
County Kildare
Ireland
www.theteenagersbookoflife.com

All rights © 2020 Tony Griffin

Paperback	ISBN: 978 1 78846 175 7
eBook – mobi format	ISBN: 978 1 78846 176 4
eBook – ePub format	ISBN: 978 1 78846 177 1
Amazon paperback edition	ISBN: 978 1 78846 178 8

All rights reserved. No part of this book may be reproduced or utilised in any form or by any means electronic or mechanical, including photocopying, filming, recording, video recording, photography, or by any information storage and retrieval system, nor shall by way of trade or otherwise be lent, resold or otherwise circulated in any form of binding or cover other than that in which it is published without prior permission in writing from the publisher.

The right of Tony Griffin to be identified as the author of the work has been asserted by him in accordance with the Copyright, Designs and Patents Act 1988.

Produced by Kazoo Independent Publishing Services
222 Beech Park, Lucan, Co. Dublin
www.kazoopublishing.com

Kazoo Independent Publishing Services is not the publisher of this work. All rights and responsibilities pertaining to this work remain with SoulPlace Publishing.

Kazoo offers independent authors a full range of publishing services. For further details visit www.kazoopublishing.com

Graphic design by Hazel Breen
Cover design by Andrew Brown
Printed in the EU

PATRONS

I owe a great debt of gratitude to the patrons, whose kindness turned this book from a feeling into something real and hopefully helpful.

The McDonagh family
The Robus and Slein family
Todd McDonald, Ashley Ward and the wonderful Winnie.
The Keily family

TONY GRIFFIN has always been fascinated by the human experience and has spent his life exploring this passion. In 2010 he co-authored the bestselling book *Screaming at the Sky*, which was recognised for courageously dismantling taboos around mental health. In 2011 he co-founded the Soar Foundation, a pioneering emotional and mental health organisation that focuses on developing teenagers' resilience and character.

CONTENTS

My Love Letter to You		9
Chapter 1	*Who Are You?*	11
Chapter 2	*Dreams*	39
Chapter 3	*Feelings*	55
Chapter 4	*Friends*	89
Chapter 5	*Life*	99
Chapter 6	*Hard Times*	135
Chapter 7	*Love*	165
Chapter 8	*Make It Better*	187
Chapter 9	*Your Parents Are Idiots and So Are You*	203
Chapter 10	*Death*	207
Acknowledgements		213

MY LOVE LETTER TO YOU

In this book I am going to tell you a few things you already know and a few things you may not know but need to hear. I am doing this because I love you. And because I feel you are completely undervalued by the majority of adults. As adults we forget what it was like to be a teenager and how much wisdom we carried at that time of our lives. Because adults have forgotten that wisdom and instead acquired a lot of knowledge (much of it useless), they do not see you for what you are. I want you to know that I do. I want you to know I see who you are going to become and it is incredible. In this book I am not offering you advice, only some things to consider. Do with it whatever you wish; burn the book if you want! And then go and live your life and write your own book from what you see and hear and learn about what it is to be alive.

If you decide to read this book and not burn it, then it can be whatever you need it to be. Maybe you need it to inspire you to go for whatever you want in life, or to soothe the feelings you hide around not being good enough or beautiful enough or big enough or whatever enough. Or it may just be a reminder of what you know already – that you are weird and different and that is exactly who you are going to be.

This book is a celebration of who you are and a reminder to be that for the rest of your life. It is my love letter to you, and all I wish for you is that your life will be a great adventure with twists and turns, ups and downs, heartbreak and highs and, most of all, I wish that you will always know that you are loved.

Love,
Tony.

P.S. I hope your parents read this too so they can begin to remember.

Chapter 1
WHO ARE YOU?

FOUND

Once upon a time a boy wandered the earth looking for answers. He wanted to know why we are here and what this thing called life is. After years searching, he got lost in a forest. It was nighttime and he had nowhere to sleep. He was afraid. He wanted to give up. Then he came across a little house deep inside the dark forest. It was his only hope, so he knocked on the door. The door opened, and a warm and welcoming light shone from inside. An old man and an old woman stood at the door and smiled at the young boy.

"I'm lost and have nowhere to stay tonight," the boy said quietly, feeling a heavy tiredness.

The old man and the old woman looked at each other, nodded and turned to the boy. "We have been waiting for you," the old man said. "Let us show you to a room where you can rest, and in the morning you can tell us about your adventures."

The next morning the boy awoke to feel the light shining through the window. The old man and the old woman had breakfast ready, and when the boy had eaten as much as he could – for he was very hungry after his long trip – the old man said, "So, tell us all that you have seen on your travels."

For hours the boy told the couple of all he had seen and experienced. They smiled and nodded and enjoyed hearing about the boy's adventures. Finally the old woman asked the boy if he had found what he was looking for on his search around the world.

The boy told her he had not, that his questions about why we are here and what this thing called life is were still unanswered.

Then the old woman's face became serious and she said to the boy, "You have been travelling for a long time, and because you are one of our tribe, we are going to help you find your way." Then she told him this story:

> There once was a tigress who was about to give birth. One day, when she was out hunting, she came upon a herd of goats. She gave chase and, even in her condition, managed to kill one of them. But the stress of the chase forced her into labour, and she died as she gave birth to a male cub. The goats, who had run away, returned when they sensed that the danger was over. Approaching the dead tigress, they discovered her newborn cub and adopted him into their herd.
>
> The tiger cub grew up among the goats believing he, too, was a goat. He bleated as well as he could, he smelled like a goat and ate only vegetation; in every respect he behaved like a goat. Yet within him beat the heart of a tiger.
>
> All went well until the day an old tiger approached the goat herd and attacked and killed one of the goats. The rest of the goats ran away as soon as they saw the old tiger, but our young tiger saw no reason to run away, for he sensed no danger.
>
> Although the old tiger had been on many hunts, he had never in his life been as shocked as he was when he came across the young tiger. He didn't know what to make of this tiger who smelled like a goat, bleated like a goat and in every way acted like a goat. Being a rather rough old duffer, and not particularly sympathetic, the old tiger grabbed the young one by the scruff of the neck, dragged him to a nearby creek and showed him his reflection in the water. But the young tiger was unimpressed with his own reflection; it meant nothing to him and he failed to see his similarity to the old tiger.
>
> Frustrated by the young tiger's lack of comprehension, the old tiger dragged him back to the place where he had made his kill. There he ripped a piece of meat from the dead goat and shoved it into the mouth of the young tiger. At first the young tiger gagged and tried spitting out the flesh, but the old tiger was determined to show the young one

who he really was and he made sure the cub swallowed the food. When he was sure the cub had swallowed it all, the old tiger shoved another piece of meat into him, and this time there was a change.

Our young tiger now allowed himself to taste the raw flesh and warm blood, and he ate this piece with gusto. When he finished chewing, the young tiger stretched, and then, for the first time in his young life, he let out a powerful roar – the roar of the jungle cat. Then the two tigers disappeared into the forest.

The boy was silent for some time as he tried to make sense of the story. Part of him was angry. He was about to give up his search, and here he was being told a story about a tiger who thought he was a goat. He didn't have a clue what it meant. Thinking that the couple had been very kind to him, he swallowed his anger and asked the old woman to explain what the story meant.

And so she went on: "Each of us is born into the world a unique human being. We are born with DNA that decides our fingerprint, what we look like and even maps out some of our behaviour. We are also born with something special to us that no one else has – you can call it your zing or your spirit or your soul. It is that special something that defines you and will be with you throughout your life. Let's call it your soul-print.

"When we are born we are completely defenceless. We stare into our mother's and father's eyes and depend on them for everything. We cannot do anything for ourselves. We would die without being fed, changed, cared for by those around us. We are completely vulnerable. To make sure we are not hurt and that we are taken care of, we develop a personality that both keeps us safe and makes others like us so that they will protect us. As we develop this personality that keeps us safe in the world, we try to fit in and adapt to the world around us. We follow the rules of the society we are born into. We do things that will please our parents. We begin to understand that if we act in certain ways, we will get approval, and if we act in other ways, we will feel the sting of disapproval or punishment and so get back in line. This is valuable; otherwise we might not survive beyond childhood. However, during this process of growing up and fitting in, something else occurs which is dangerous in the long run."

"What is that?" asked the boy, hanging on the old woman's every word.

"As we adapt to the world around so we will fit in, following the rules of the family and society we are born into, we move away from our soul-print and forget who we really are. We come to believe we are the personality we developed to stay safe and be accepted. We believe we are goats, when in reality the truth is that we have the beating heart of a tiger. We are more than we think we are, and deep down every one of us knows this to be true. Some people, like you, go in search of this something. Others will call you crazy, a fool, even irresponsible, but deep down they know that they too have a tiger's heart. They have just denied the truth."

"I have gone on this search," the boy said, "but I do not feel I have found what you are talking about. I am beginning to believe those people who called me a fool were right. I feel more lost than ever. If this soul-print exists, how do I find it? How do I remember who I really am?"

The old woman looked the boy straight in the eye. Her face changed to a kind expression that made the boy want to cry. "You have not found it because you were looking in the wrong place," she said. "You were looking outside yourself, when all along what you have been looking for is on the inside.

"We will show you the way back," the old woman continued, "and then you can show others."

Then the old man said, "We were right. He is one of us."

And the old woman smiled in agreement.

The Goat/Tiger story above is sourced from the book *Embracing Ourselves*. Copyright © 1989, by Hal Stone and Sidra Stone. Reprinted with permission of New World Library, Novato, CA. www.newworldlibrary.com

WHO ARE YOU?

Are you your name?

Where you come from?

What you have achieved, done or seen?

Are you the stories you tell about yourself to fit in?

Are you the rules your parents said you have to follow?

The things that have happened to you, good and bad?

Are you your clothes, jewellery, phone, watch?

The school you go to, who you hang out with?

Well, who the hell are you?

Are you all of these? Is that who you are?

Or

Are you more?

Is there something to you that no one else has? Have you a one-in-the-universe soul-print that can never be copied, a barcode that will never die, that no shotgun or bomb or hurtful comment can ever extinguish?

What if you were more than you think you are, but you've forgotten?

What if it was time to remember?

TO BE YOUNG IS TO BE NIMBLE. WE CHANGE QUICKLY. WE CRAVE CONNECTION. WE PLAY. WE ARE EMOTIONAL BEINGS. WE ARE ROMANTIC. WE ARE ARTISTIC. WE LAUGH. WE ARE PASSIONATE. WE HAVE ENTHUSIASM AND ENERGY. WE REBEL. WE QUESTION. WE ARE HONEST. WE ARE MALLEABLE. WE HAVE HOPE. WE ARE NAIVE OF DANGERS. WE TAKE RISKS. WE HAVE ZEST FOR LIFE. WE CRAVE PHYSICAL CONNECTION. WE MAKE NOISE. WE FALL IN LOVE EASILY. WE HAVE DREAMS. WE BELIEVE. WE CARE DEEPLY. WE ARE CRAZY. WE JOKE. WE LIVE IN A WORLD OF FIRSTS AND POSSIBILITY.

— TOM HARKIN

YOUR PAST DOES NOT DEFINE YOU. BUT UNDERSTANDING WHERE YOU HAVE COME FROM, WHO HAS SHAPED YOU AND THE CONTOURS OF YOUR STORY CAN GUIDE YOU INTO A THOUSAND TOMORROWS.

YOUR TRIBE'S FAMILY TREE

Your family tree is a bloodline that stretches back to the beginning of time. It is a story of all the people who have gone before you and all those still alive that are rocking this life with you today.

One thing we gain from seeing the map of our tribe's bloodline is the realisation that we are not alone. We come from a long line of people who are watching over us, like the stars in the sky, and they are on our side.

Fill in the diagram on the next page to trace your own bloodline. Try to go back as far as you can.

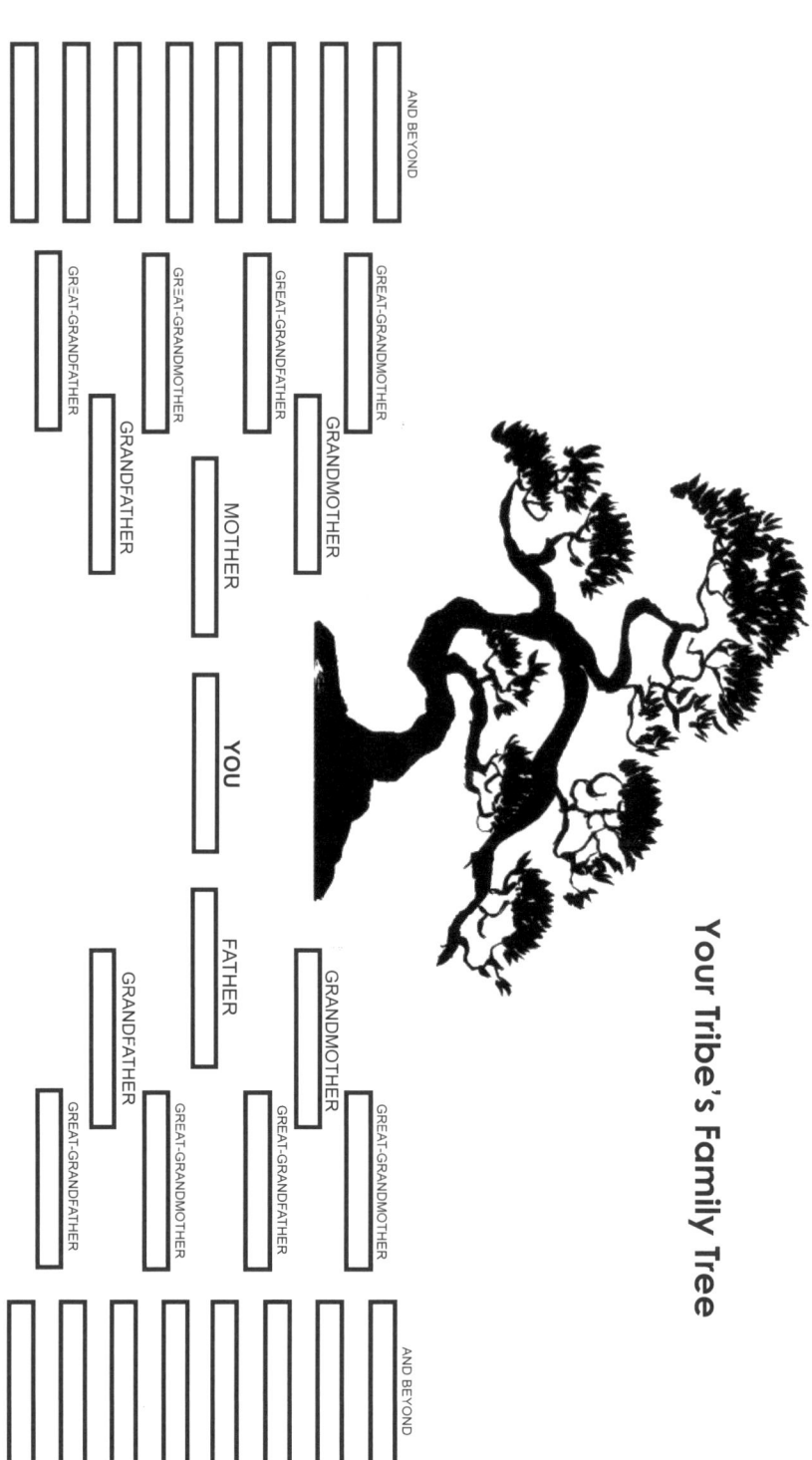

EXPLORING YOUR BLOODLINE

Some of us are born into loving families, some of us into loveless ones that nevertheless satisfy our basic needs of food and shelter. Others are born into chaos and pain. Whatever the world you arrived into looks and feels like, you are here for a reason, and it's time to discover what that reason is and where this life can take you. One way to do this is to tap the vein of your bloodline to answer the question "Who am I?" And to do that we must time-travel.

> **WISDOM IS NOT FOUND IN YEARS LIVED BUT IN EXPERIENCES HAD. HOWEVER, THE LONGER WE HAVE LIVED THE MORE OPPORTUNITIES WE HAVE TO EXPERIENCE LIFE AND LEARN ITS SECRETS.**

CALL TO ACTION

Find the oldest relative you feel would be up for it and ask if you can interview them. I want you to help your grandad, grandmother or any older member of your tribe (one you really like and feel comfortable with) express the wisdom they've gained during their precious life. If you don't have any older relatives, ask an older person you like and care about.

Play chat-show host, and either in person or online, ask them the questions listed below! You can fill in the blanks or just enjoy the chat.

Tell me about what life was like for you when you were my age.
_____
_____
_____

If you knew my mum/dad when they were my age, what were they like as a teenager?
_____
_____
_____

What is the hardest challenge or experience you've faced in your life?
_____
_____
_____

Do you have any regrets?
_____
_____
_____

What advice would you give to your teenage self?
_____
_____
_____

Who was your first love?
_____
_____

Can you tell me your happiest memory?
_____
_____
_____

Age is not the only way we build wisdom. So ask yourself if there was any advice your interviewee gave their teenage self that you would not agree with. Or was there something you would like to put into action now for yourself?

ROMY AND BEAR

Hi! My name is Romy. I'm five-and-a-half, nearly six, actually. This is my little brother, Bear. He's only half a year old. Our mum and dad don't know this but we can talk to each other, even though I am way older and have lived so much longer. We speak a language that grown-ups don't know. It's called Googish and everybody loses it at different ages. When I talk Googish to Bear, I tell him everything I have learned about life, and I've learned so much that I'm very wise, actually.

Bear and I talk about everything and I tell him what to expect as he gets closer to being older like me. Bear reminds me to never forget who I really am. Listen up, because I am going to translate our Googish talks and you can listen in, so you can remember who you are too.

BEAR: Romy, who am I now that I am on earth?

ROMY: You are my little brother and your name is Bear. I wanted someone to be my brother or sister and I wished for you, and God said, "Here you go!" You are with me and Momma and Dadda now and you are safe.

BEAR: It is very different here from where I came from. Before I came here I was an angel. But I am glad I picked you and Momma and Dadda as my family. I have missed you.

ROMY: I've missed you too. Oh, the fun we will have, Bear! I'll tell you everything I've learned in the long five-and-a-half years I have been here on earth.

BEAR: Oh, how lovely, Romy! And I'll remind you about what you have forgotten since you left heaven.

THE MOST IMPORTANT RELATIONSHIP YOU'LL EVER HAVE IN YOUR LIFE IS WITH YOURSELF. EVERY OTHER IS SECONDARY.

HEAD

You learn things with your head, and a head is a very handy thing. It is like your phone's operating system. You don't see it working away in the background, but without it you'd be fucked. But it's not the source of your magic.

HEART

Your heart has an intelligence all of its own. And how you hear it is . . .

Be quiet and still.

Go to the woods.

Watch the ocean.

Listen to the wind.

Run as fast as you can down a grassy hill in a rainstorm.

Scream at the starry sky as you walk home from a night out with your friend.

Feel the touch of someone you love with all your heart.

SOUL

Your soul knows the way. It has a plan for you and can conjure up the miracles your head can't even dream of. Your soul will never leave you. It is always in your corner and knows the way home.

WE NEED ALL THREE

You can get through life with just your head, but you will never feel alive without heeding your soul's whisper and listening to your heart's call.

Heart trumps head all day long.

ROMY AND BEAR TALK ABOUT HEART

BEAR: Romy, when you hug me I feel a warm feeling from my head to my toes and all the way deep inside. Big brother, what is it I am feeling?

ROMY: That's your heart, Bear.

BEAR: What is my heart?

ROMY: Your heart is the lovely feeling place that goes "RING, RING!" when you are with someone you love more than anything.

BEAR: Yes, that's it. That's how I feel when you, Momma and Dadda look down at me when I am lying on my favourite blanket. I feel the "RING RING!" feeling way deep down inside my heart.

ROMY: So do I, Bear, so do I.

BEAR: I love having a big brother like you who knows everything, Romy.

VOYAGER, TELL ME WHAT'VE YOU SEEN

In the beginning human beings lived in small, isolated groups. When a stranger appeared on the horizon, fear filled the hearts of those anxiously watching from their settlement. When the stranger reached the perimeter of the settlement, the fiercest warriors and the leader of the settlement went to meet them. First they had to know the stranger did not intend to harm them. After they had satisfied themselves that the stranger posed no risk, they always asked the same two questions.

WHERE DID YOU COME FROM?

WHAT HAVE YOU SEEN?

Before social media, before TV and radio and newspapers, this was how people learned about what lay beyond the mountains, on the other side of the ocean and deep inside the dark forest.

I want to ask you the same question. What have you seen that no other person in the history of human kind has seen? What have you felt that has never been felt? When you go back to the place we all come from, what will you take with you that has marked the trajectory of your life? On the next page there is an almost impossible exercise. I want you to tell the story of your life through three lines.

CALL TO ACTION

Imagine you have been told you have a week to live and you need to tell the story of your life. This story will last forever and tell the tale of your time on earth. Don't hold back. Write in pencil, so if you're afraid of it being read, you can erase it and it's your secret forever.

HOW YOU DO IT

The top blue line tracks the **epic highs** of your life – the moments that took your breath away. These are the precious memories that have been the amazing experiences of your life. Perhaps it is the birth of a brother or sister, a special family holiday, the first time you fell in love. Track them through your life from as far back as you can remember right up to today.

The middle beige line tracks the moments that have no strong feelings associated with them – the **blah moments** that were neither highs nor lows.

The bottom red line tracks the **heart-wrenching lows** of your life. These are the moments in your life that have hurt. They were painful to live through and it might even sting to remember them now. You know the ones – the death of someone you loved, parents divorcing, losing a friend, a period you thought you wouldn't make it through. You might even be experiencing a heart-wrenching low in your life right now. Again, track from as far back as you can remember right up to today.

After you've added the moments, join the dots through time.

Here's what mine looks like.

Fill out your Life Line on the lines below, use mine to help guide you

Here is a snapshot of mine...

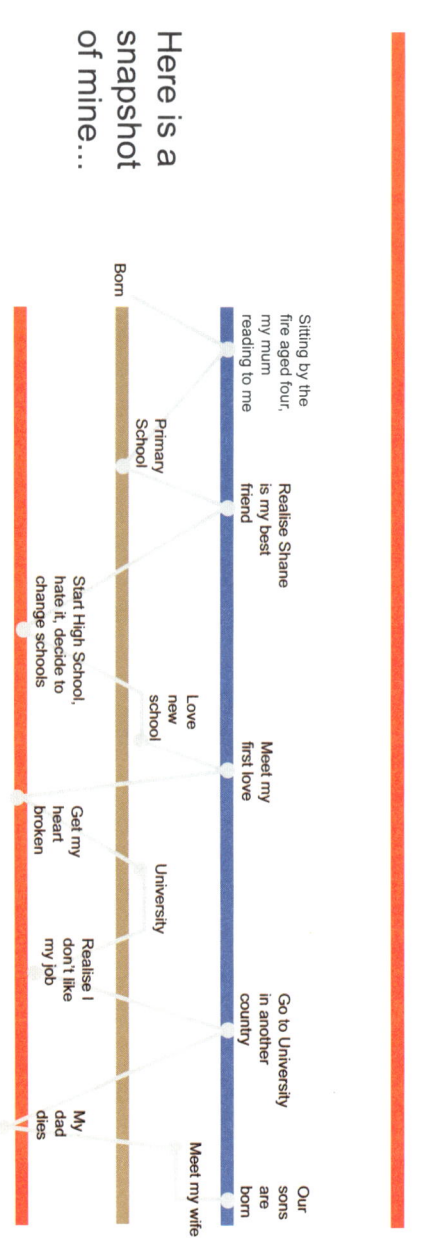

- Born
- Sitting by the fire aged four, my mum reading to me
- Primary School
- Realise Shane is my best friend
- Start High School, hate it, decide to change schools
- Love new school
- Meet my first love
- Get my heart broken
- University
- Realise I don't like my job
- Go to University in another country
- My dad dies
- Meet my wife
- Our sons are born

How did it feel seeing the life you have lived on one page? Was it all epic highs or heart-wrenching lows? Or was it a mix of both and your line was like a recurring wave? It doesn't matter how it looked – it can be clean and tidy or as messy as elephant saliva.

When we look back on our life, we don't necessarily remember everything that happened. We remember it in moments. We store the most significant memories that had a particularly emotional beat that set them apart. We remember times in our lives based on how we felt at that time. The stronger the feelings, the more we remember it.

Say you are one of those strangers who has wandered into an isolated settlement in ancient times. They are nice people. They welcome you to their group, they have a great Spotify playlist with banging tunes and they have the best snacks. They ask you to answer three questions about your life so they can really know who you are:

- » Who is your hero?

- » What was the hardest time of your life or the hardest thing you have faced?

- » What has been the greatest high-point of your life?

You can pull these from the life story you did earlier, or if you decided not to write it down, this is another opportunity. Remember the reason we are doing this is so you can remember that you are wiser than you may even realise. And by unearthing this wisdom, you get to be the master of what you decide to do with your life.

On the next page I've shared my answers to the same three questions.

Hero: My mother. She had a tough childhood. She left a place she knew to come to a country she didn't so that her children could have the life she felt in her heart was going to be good for them. She had seven children. She worked nights in a retirement home to make sure that we had the opportunity to do whatever we dreamed of. One night I sat on the stairs in our house crying because acne had exploded on my face like a vicious swarm of wasps had attacked me. I thought I was ugly, but my mother reminded me that this would pass and that a great life was waiting for me. I didn't believe her at the time but she was right.

Hardest time: My father dying and not getting to say goodbye to him. My father died from cancer. I was living abroad and didn't get home before he passed away. My mother and six brothers and sisters were there to say goodbye. I wasn't. I really regretted it and it haunted me. It sent me to a dark place.

Highest point(s): The birth of our sons. My wife and I have two sons. I can't describe how I felt when they were handed to me. With the first, it felt surreal, like an out-of-body experience. With the second, I felt relief. I couldn't be in the delivery room and instead paced the floor in a tiny waiting room. Suddenly from down the hall I heard the cry of a baby. I wanted to break down the door to see if it was our baby. I asked a nurse to check for me. She went away to see. She was gone a while and I started to panic. Was there something wrong? Was my wife OK? Was there something they didn't want to tell me? Did our baby make it? After what seemed like an eternity, she came back to tell me that my wife was OK and that our new son was healthy. A few minutes later he was handed to me. I have never felt such relief in my life, just knowing everything was OK.

CALL TO ACTION

Be as brave and honest as you can. Who is your hero? Why are they your hero? What has been the hardest time of your life and what was it like to go through? What has been the highest point of your life, and how did it make you feel? Use a pencil if you want so you can rub it out afterwards and no one need ever see it.

My hero:_____
_____
_____
_____
_____

My hardest time:_____
_____
_____
_____
_____

My highest point: _____
_____
_____
_____
_____

USE YOUR WISDOM

One of the things adults forget about being a teenager is that already you have experienced life in all its beauty and maybe in all its devastating darkness too. When we stop and take the time to understand the road we have walked to be where we are today, we realise that we are wiser than we give ourselves credit for. You have wisdom locked inside you and now it's time to pull it up from the depths and take it with you on the journey ahead.

CALL TO ACTION

What have you learned about who you are, about people and about the world from what you have seen and experienced in your life up to now? Dig deep into your soul to bring your wisdom to the surface.

_____
_____
_____
_____
_____

Chapter 2
DREAMS

ROMY AND BEAR TALK ABOUT DREAMS

ROMY: Have you heard of dreams?

BEAR: No, big brother, I haven't heard of dreams. Is it something you eat?

ROMY: Ha! No, Bear. Dreams are things you want to do or be, or places you want to go.

BEAR: And how do I get to this dreams place?

ROMY: You get there by following your heart.

BEAR: How do I follow my heart?

ROMY: You go really quiet and you just listen to it. It takes practice, and the grown-ups have forgotten how to do it because they only listen to their heads. Your head screams and tells you what it's afraid of, but your heart whispers so you must be very still so you can hear it. I still remember how to listen to my heart. That's the way you get there, little brother, and I'm going to teach you.

DISCOVER YOUR ZING

Your zing is the real you, the you who no one else could dream of being. It has been called many names – heart, soul, essence. It's the piece of meteorite dust that you are, that no one else can copy. The sad thing is that as people grow up, they often lose touch with their zing and feel that they are not good enough. Really, the purpose of life is to rediscover your zing over and over again.

Some adults say that having dreams is wishy-washy shit, that dreams are for children, or something you do when you're asleep, and you should grow up and live in the real world. I think that's the saddest thing I've ever heard. The truth is that dreams are a serious business. They are life and death. Because if you don't have dreams, you die while still living, and that's the worst thing of all – to be walking dead. Dreams are more important than oxygen, because having a dream, following its trail, is the way back to your zing. And remember, finding your zing is the reason you're here.

ZING

Dreams are the inner magnet that lead you to your zing. They pull you in the direction that your heart and soul want to go. Your mind will come up with every reason why you should be careful and not allow the magnet tp pull you where it wants you to go. This is because the Law of Dreams is that they test you by revealing how much you had inside you all along but perhaps could not see. In the end, dreams make you STRONG because they first make you feel WEAK, SCARED and LOST. But when you keep going, you realise that you have survived, and deep down you know that you refused to surrender to your fears and you lived to tell the tale – all because you didn't give up on your dreams.

In the end, when you have chased your dreams and they have kicked the shit out of you and you have held on and survived, you'll realise that the dreams were never the most important thing at all. The most important thing was who you became along the way, how much your dreams helped you to remember who you really are.

WHAT YOU NEED TO KNOW ABOUT DREAMS

- » Your dreams are the way to rediscover your zing.

- » Your dreams have their origin in what you love to do.

- » They are what bring you the most joy.

- » Following your dream will test you again and again.

- » The people you love may not understand it.

- » In school you probably won't be taught about how to get to your dreams, so don't expect someone else to set you on the path.

- » Having dreams isn't like drinking. There is no age you have to reach to be allowed to get into it.

- » Your dreams will break your heart.

- » Your dreams will make you feel like you could die trying to achieve them.

- » You might want to die along the way.

- » Your dream will change shape again and again, so you must keep listening with your heart and your soul. They know the way.

And remember – the dream is just the vehicle. If you get the dream and are an asshole, then you didn't get it!

CALL TO ACTION

- » Did you ever have a dream and chase it?

- » Did you ever have a dream and it died along the way because you thought you were not enough or that people would laugh at you?

Oh, and another thing: don't make money your dream. That's one sure way to get the dream but miss the magic. I know lots of millionaires who are miserable. Choose dreams that come from what you love, from things that make you feel alive. Then you'll get good at the thing you love and someone, somewhere, will want to pay you to do that thing you love. If you chase money as your primary dream, it's like leaning your ladder against a wall and climbing to the top. When you reach the top of the ladder and look out on the view, you'll realise it was leaning against the wrong wall all along.

The right wall for you is the one that makes you feel like you would climb the ladder for free. Your parents might not agree with this. Your guidance counsellor or teachers may not either. But don't worry about that. Most of them are half-dead, walking around like zombies already, and they're not as wise as you (because no one told them this early in their life). I'm not saying money isn't important – it is. But it's not the most important thing in life, so choose a dream you love, not one that will make you rich.

Whatever you do, whatever dream you chase, **do it with goddamn spirit**!

YOUR DREAM DOES NOT MATTER

...as much as who you become along the way

WE ARE ALL EQUAL, BUT WE ARE NOT ALL BORN EQUAL

There are two truths. The first is that we are all souls, all pieces of the same meteorite dust that landed us on earth. The second truth is that we are not all born into equal circumstances. Some of you will have been born into a family where you have every chance to rise to the top of whatever area you desire. Some of you will be born in to families where you have to fight through shit just to stay alive, never mind finding your dream and following its magnetic pull. I am not going to tell you that you can do whatever you want, because your truth right now might be that the odds are stacked against you, and maybe you can't see a way out. But I do want to tell you that where you are at this moment is not where you need to end up. We are all here for a reason, whether we are born into opportunity or into a fight.

If you were born into a fight . . .

- » I want you to know that you have something about you no one else has.
- » I want you to know YOU are here for a reason.
- » I want you to know there is a way out of where you are.

You might need to hide your dream and care for it for a while in case someone destroys it but you have AS MUCH RIGHT to dream as anyone else, so you dream and keep it close to your heart and no matter what shit you need to wade through to get there, DO NOT GIVE UP!

GOING AGAINST THE FLOW

Going against the flow and sticking with your dreams is often the road less travelled. One person who has done this is the singer-songwriter and creative force Frank Ocean.

Music was always Frank's thing. In high school he began recording music, working various jobs to pay for studio time. When Hurricane Katrina destroyed the studio where he was creating his music, he didn't give up. He threw himself into what he wanted to do and moved closer to where he thought he could get his break. Eventually he found the success he was working toward when his album *Channel Orange* won him heaps of awards.

But the fact that he stuck with his dream till he caught up with it isn't the bravest thing about Frank Ocean. When he got there, he told the world that his first love was a man. His courageous decision to open up about his sexuality shocked many because of the historically homophobic nature of the rap-music industry. There was risk involved in his honesty, and Frank acknowledged this at the time when he said, "I don't know what happens now, and that's all right. I don't have any secrets I need kept anymore. I feel like a free man."

He always saw new possibilities, and using his platform to encourage acceptance and love was another way for him to storm the barricades and shine his light into the world. Frank is going to help you go mining for all the potential that exists inside you so that you can align your own piece of the universe with your destiny.

LET'S TIME-TRAVEL

Once on a plane Frank wrote a letter to himself of five years earlier. He encouragesd himself not to lose faith in his search for his path. He tells himself that he will have to work some shit jobs to get by and that he will get fired from them, that his girlfriend will break up with him and that he will have his heart broken. But he tells himself that some amazing things are going to happen for him. He will pour his heartbreak into his music and create an album the world wants to hear because it will speak to people's souls. He tells himself to be patient and to be good to people and promises himself that it is going to work. He even lets himself in on the secret that the plane he is on is taking him to work with Kanye West and Jay-Z. He ends the letter by saying, "It's all working out, kid. You made it."

Sometimes to know where we want to go it can help to remember how far we have come. It's the way we learn to trust ourselves and know that in the end there are no wrong choices. So let's go back in time.

CALL TO ACTION

Inspired by Frank Ocean's letter to himself, write to yourself way back when you were five years younger. Give younger you an insight into what's coming down the tracks for them. Explain where you are now and maybe reassure them that everything is going to be OK. What age were you five years ago? What was going on? Who were your friends? Are they still your mates? What music were you into? Do you still live in the same place?

_____
_____
_____
_____
_____
_____

NOW LET'S TIME-TRAVEL INTO THE FUTURE

If you were to time-travel five years into the future to find you have already smashed some of your dreams, what would that look like? Go crazy here. Like, really crazy. Then rip it out and stick it on your bedroom wall. Then just let destiny show you the way. If you would prefer to just close your eyes and imagine your dream future, then go for it. Do this your way. As you create your dream future, think about what you know you are naturally really good at and what you are interested in. Think about where these things might take you if anything were possible. And I mean *anything*.

Here are some questions to fire up your time travelling.

In five years' time, if anything were possible, you knew you could not fail and you were fearless, what would you be doing?
_____
_____
_____

How would you like to feel about yourself in five years' time?
_____
_____
_____

Where in the world would your dream have brought you, and who would be with you?
_____
_____
_____

What relationship would you like to be better, and what does that relationship feel like in the future you are seeing?
_____
_____
_____

COMFORT ZONES

Adults are great at giving advice they read in a book or saw in an Insta story. One thing they will tell you to do is to get out of your comfort zone. Most of them don't even understand what they're talking about. So I'm not going to tell you clichéd shit about getting out of your comfort zone because that's where the magic happens. Puke!

The truth is I feel like I have been frightened all my life. So I'm not going to tell you to smash your comfort zone every day because that's the only way to live. But what I do want you to know is that you have more in you than you can even imagine, and it will never come out and change your world if you're too afraid. Find ways to scare yourself in life and you'll find things that you've never dreamed of happen. So try stuff. Except when it is just smart for you to say no. Like when you know something is just bad for you and will leave you feeling like the darkest world just rolled into town. Friends/boyfriends/girlfriends who make you feel bad or "less than you know you are" is a good example. Whatever you do, if it makes you feel like shit then move the hell on and don't get stuck there. Better stuff is waiting for you.

ROMY AND BEAR TALK MORE ABOUT DREAMS

BEAR: What's your dream, Romy?

ROMY: To never forget who I am, little brother.

BEAR: Me too. We can help each other never forget.

ROMY: That sounds good, Bear.

BEAR: Romy, why do adults forget who they are as they grow up? Why do they forget that they are a bit of the magic meteorite dust?

ROMY: Well, they get all serious and want to look perfect. So they get a serious face and a serious job and they forget what they love. And then it's bye-bye magic meteorite dust. But not all of them are like that.

BEAR: Really? Some don't forget?

ROMY: Everyone forgets Bear, but some adults remember. And you know these ones because their eyes are sparkly like ours and they laugh at themselves a lot. I like those grown-ups the most.

BEAR: Oh, big brother, we'll make sure our eyes always shine and we laugh at each other.

ROMY: No, they laugh at themselves, Bear!

BEAR: Ah! Well, then we will always laugh at ourselves and each other! Shiny-eyed brothers till the end, Romy.

ROMY: Shiny-eyed brothers till the end, Bear.

Chapter 3
FEELINGS

WHEN THINGS GET TOO MUCH

Sometimes when you are out there doing your thing, slaying dragons, life can become too much. Do you ever feel that way? Overwhelmed? I do. As a kid I had a place I used to go to in the fields across from my house. I would walk through the grassy hills with a stick and my dog, who I loved. There was one spot with a big rock stuck in the ground that was shaped like a horse. I would climb on it and sing to myself and to the trees. I loved those moments away from my brothers and sisters and the chaos of home.

A few years ago I had a dream of cycling from one side of Canada to the other. It was 7,000 km, and when the idea came to me I had no bike and very little cycling experience. At first my family weren't jumping up and down in support of my dream. Of course this was only because they were afraid for me because they loved me!

Then one day my mother sent me this note:

> Ships were meant to sail the seas. They were not meant to be tied up in the harbour. Perhaps, if there is a stormy sea and the waves are crashing, then they need to come into the harbour and rest and stay safe. But they were not BUILT to stay in the harbour.

What she was saying was as much as she loved me and wanted to protect me, she was giving her blessing for me to chase my dream. She was encouraging me to go to sea. I did, and it was the best experience of my life.

The cycle across Canada was in memory of my father – one last attempt to make him proud of me. I was desperately sad and lonely when he died. I had regrets. On the cycle I had long periods of time on my own. I thought about my dad. I talked to him. And I wept at his passing and because I wouldn't see him again till it was my turn to go. After the cycle I went through a period of darkness. I couldn't get out of bed; I felt awkward in crowds; I had no energy. Everything seemed like too much and I felt overwhelmed all of the time. At the time I had no answers to the questions I am going to ask you now.

When things are getting on top of you, and you feel smothered by life, what do you do to find some space?

When the waves are crashing all around and you think you will fall overboard, how do you stay in the race?

What do you do to stay alive to fight another day?

One of my answers is on the next page . . .

SAY, "FUCK OFF, WORLD!" AND HEAD TO THE WOODS WITH A STICK.

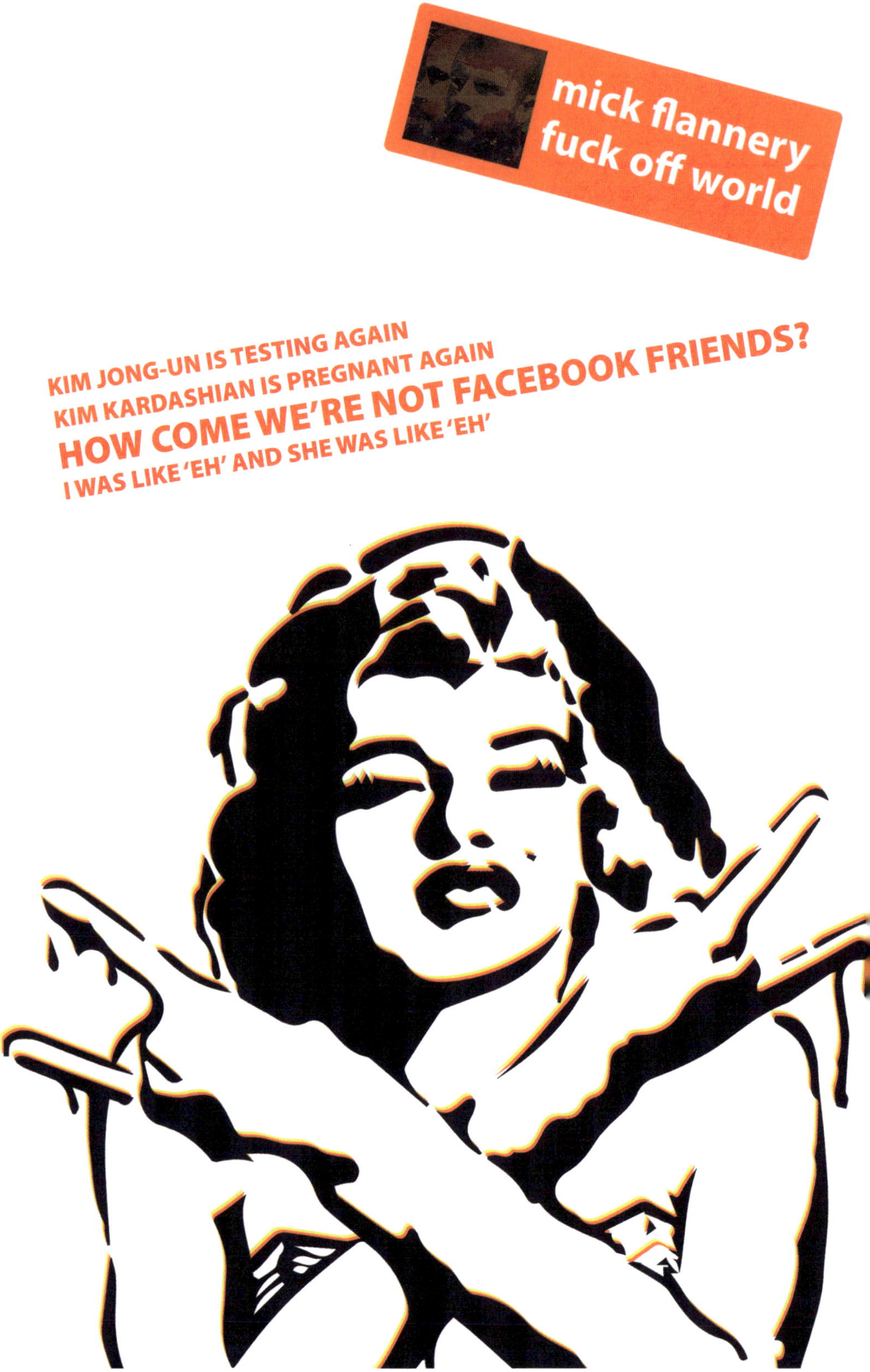

KIM JONG-UN IS TESTING AGAIN
KIM KARDASHIAN IS PREGNANT AGAIN
HOW COME WE'RE NOT FACEBOOK FRIENDS?
I WAS LIKE 'EH' AND SHE WAS LIKE 'EH'

FUCK OFF WORLD

Kim Jong-Un is testing again

Kim Kardashian is pregnant again

How come we're not facebook friends?

I was like "eh" and she was like "eh"

Fuck off world, fuck off politics, I'm goin' in the woods with a stick

I'm goin' by the stream just to sit

It's fun out here, berries in a sack

No banker walkin' round that wants his money back

No one spreading lies, no one selling guns

Nothing to advertise, no capitalism

Open ear to the earthly sound

Open arm to the rain come down

Singin' fuck off world, fuck off politics, I'm goin' in the woods with a stick

I'm goin' by the stream just to sit

And I know I'm supposed to think about injustice

I know I'm supposed to fight the good fight

I know I'm supposed to care about progress

But with all of that in mind tonight, you might

Fuck off world, fuck off politics, I'm goin' in the woods with a stick

I'm goin' by the stream just to sit

Generation snowflake, fuck off

Left-wing right-wing, fuck off

Twitter feed face, fuck off

Instagram page, fuck oahohahohahoff

WHEN YOU NEED TO SAY, "FUCK OFF, WORLD!"

It is harder now than ever before to be on your own when you want to be. And that is why we need it more than ever. Our Snapchat and Instagram feeds can make us feel like our life is shit and everyone else is living the dream. When you feel like you need to say "Fuck off, world!" how do you do it?

Here are a few ideas:

- » Climb a hill or a mountain and scream "I am alive" at the top of your lungs.

- » Dive into the sea in your clothes. (Actually, don't! People will call the fire brigade. Do it naked instead!)

- » Put in your earphones and play your favourite tunes. Lock the bathroom or bedroom door and dance like you're possessed by your alter ego, the one who's an incredible dancer.

- » Walk along the beach and collect stones and shells that call out to you.

- » Play with your pet and tell them everything you are worried about. They won't talk back or tell you to get over it!

P.S.: Turn off your phone while you're telling the world to fuck off. And don't have it in your hand if you dive into the sea naked!

P.P.S.: A big thank you to one of the greatest poets and artists in the world, Mick Flannery, for the use of the lyrics to "Fuck Off World".

HAVE A LAUGH AND GET PERSPECTIVE

HAVE A LAUGH

One of the greatest antidotes to when you feel overwhelmed by the world is to laugh. Laughter is like sorcery. It weaves spells like nothing else can. My friend Ben is the best person I know in the world for having a laugh and seeing the funny side of life. It must be because a great big dog tried to rip his face off!

When Ben was born, he was six weeks premature and had three holes in his heart. When he was seven, a dog wanted Ben's teddy bear blanket just as much as he did. They had a fight and the dog won. Ben ended up having to get hundreds of stitches all over his face to return him to the handsome kid he was before the tussle over the blanket.

Ben's superpower is that he knows how to laugh at himself and the world. We would be studying for an exam and he would just say something funny and crack me up.

Sometimes when life is getting on top of you, the best thing you can do is to laugh at it all. Like this: "Wow, I know I'm gay. I'm cool with that. But my mother is weirded out by anyone who is gay! Oh, how good is that?"

Or this: "My best friend, who I thought had my back, turns out to be so two-faced he could get a part in the next Batman movie! And he knows all my deepest darkest secrets and will probably tell the whole school about my porn addiction! Ha!"

You get my drift. Sometimes the only thing to do is to see the absurd humour in the craziness of life because that gives you some perspective and room to consider your next move.

GET PERSPECTIVE

When we take things – life, relationships, sport, school or whatever – too seriously, we choke the life out of life. We make it so do-or-die that we become emotionally overinvested in whatever's going on and how it will turn out. Some of the things I thought were the worst things that could ever happen turned out to be amazing. They were just disguised as some voodoo shit that I was overthinking and then getting stressed about. So get yourself a super-sized takeaway of perspective any time you're freaking out and think the world is about to end.

You get perspective when you realise that every feeling you've ever had has passed and all the ones to come will pass too. So when you feel like whatever is happening is a catastrophe, ask yourself this: is it as bad as standing in front of the entire school about to give a speech, trembling with nerves, and realising just as you start to give the speech that your light-grey school pants have just turned dark grey and that you feel a warm sensation on your legs?

The thing is, whatever's happening, however bad it is, if you can see that it will pass and be history one day, and you can find a way to laugh at it, in the end it's just another scene in the movie of your life. And one day you'll look back and it won't feel as big and important as it does now. So instead of waiting, why not do it now? Do a Ben on it and laugh at the shit that you used to freak out about.

What in your life seemed like something pretty terrible at the time but turned out to be a blessing in disguise that led to something good?

_____
_____
_____
_____
_____

When you are feeling overwhelmed by life or a situation, what do you do to get back on track? What has worked for you in the past?

_____
_____
_____
_____
_____

CONTROL

We feel safer when we feel in control of what's going on. Sometimes when you feel overwhelmed by life or a situation, just knowing the things you can control and those that are outside of your control is enough to allow you to breathe deeper and find peace.

Try this exercise the next time you're worried or freaking out about something. At the top of the page describe the situation. Then in one box list all the things you can change about the situation. Then in the other box list all the things about the situation that are not in your control or that you can't do anything about, at least not yet. This will help to give you a sense of control, like you are the master of your own universe for a few minutes and not a victim of circumstance. It reminds you that you have some choice about what happens next.

Situation:

_____
_____
_____
_____
_____
_____
_____
_____
_____
_____

Write the things you can control or change in the pink circle:

Write the things you cannot control or change in the yellow circle:

IF THE WALLS ARE CRASHING DOWN

Sometimes we go through something that makes us feel like the walls are about to crash down and it's not possible to laugh at the situation or see the bigger picture. Then the smartest thing you can do is reach out. When I was at my lowest I got in my car and drove around for hours. Eventually I called my sister and told her what was going on. We talked things through. She said I needed to talk to a counsellor. I thought that would make me seem weak. But I felt weak as hell already, so I decided I didn't care how it looked, that I would try it. It was the best thing I ever did. Now I look back and wonder why I waited so long to ask for help. So if you're struggling, reach out to someone you trust who you know won't judge you, or go online and find a professional to talk to. Not some weirdo who tells you that taking your clothes off on camera is the answer. No! Talk to an organisation in your country that helps people find their way back to feeling good about themselves. You won't regret it.

ROMY AND BEAR TALK ABOUT FEELINGS

BEAR: Romy, what are feelings?

ROMY: They are like a volcano inside you, Bear, and that volcano can shoot out lots of different types of lava of all different colours. Like sadness is grey, anger is dark red and happiness is bright yellow. So sometimes the lava is happy lava and sometimes it's sad lava. And sometimes they get mixed up together, and then it's just confusing.

BEAR: Why are adults so afraid of feelings, Romy?

ROMY: Because they're afraid they won't know what to do with the volcano inside them and so they never get to know the colours.

BEAR: I want to learn all the colours of the lava, Romy. Can you teach me?

ROMY: Of course, little brother. Let's start with my favourite . . .

BE YOUR OWN MASTER

One thing you will never learn in school but that you really need to know is how to be the master of your feelings. Feelings are powerful things. They cause people who are usually pretty chilled to commit murder, and they give old ladies the strength to lift cars off their grandchildren. Feelings can make you do things you thought only people on Netflix shows would do.

Feelings are crazy. They drive us . . . and yet we often find it so hard to know what we are feeling. And feelings are confusing. We can cry when we are happy and laugh when we are nervous or uncomfortable.

Because we are not taught in school how to understand our emotions, we have to find another way of doing it for ourselves. And that's hard for two reasons. First, most adults went to the same schools, which also neglected to teach them about themselves and their emotions, so they haven't a clue about their feelings and can't teach you. And second, there are some feelings that are seen by society as acceptable – happiness, excitement, etc. Society sees these as the "good" feelings. Anger, rage, jealousy, sadness, etc. are seen as "bad" feelings and treated like second-class citizens. This makes it hard to learn about the full spectrum of your emotions because you are encouraged to express some and not others.

Maybe the most important thing we will learn as humans is how to express our feelings, and especially how to express the more socially unacceptable ones. This gets personal when we feel those less-desirable emotions and we either hide them and silently feel like shit or express them in ways that make things worse. So what's the answer? First, we need to understand how we give our feelings power.

We give our feelings power when we wrap a story about what is going on around what is actually going on and the feelings that result from this are strong enough to power a small city.

For example, let's say you're not feeling great about yourself at the moment. Your friend doesn't answer your message for, like, an hour longer than usual. You feel funny about this. A thought crosses your mind like a shadow: Maybe she doesn't like me anymore. You've noticed that she's been chatting to a girl from another group and you know that they both want to go travelling to Australia. Your mam won't let you go there till you've finished college and you worry that if your friend goes without you, you'll lose touch.

Now you are starting to feel worried and a bit shit. You feel like you're going to lose your best friend. You start to look at photos on your phone of the two of you having great times and you begin to feel really bad. You think your friendship is over and you will never have good times again!

You see what sorcery occurred there? We took something fairly innocent (that actually happened to a friend of mine, and she didn't lose her best friend, but she did freak out and think she was going to) and we wrapped a story around your friend not messaging back and all of a sudden our feelings flew out of control.

What do you do when your feelings get out of control and become the executive producer, director and chief animator of your life?

First we need to understand our own feelings by getting to know them – like someone you used to see around and then became friends with. Before you didn't get them but now you know them like a best friend. Getting good at understanding your feelings makes you the master of your destiny and makes it easier for you and everyone else when you feel like you're losing your shit.

This is how you get to know your feelings and begin to understand them. You can do it regularly, especially when you feel anxious or nervous if you're, say, coming up to a big game, going to places you've never been or doing something that makes you feel scared, worried, nervous or not good enough.

The question you need to ask yourself to begin to be master of your own feelings is:

What am I feeling right now?

What are you feeling right now? Give it to me in three words.
_____ and _____ and _____ .

Come back here regularly when you feel like you're going to explode or smash your room up. Write down what you're feeling. The key is not to judge some feelings as better than others. Just notice what you are feeling and name it. No need to rush to change it straight away. It's a feeling, not an axe murderer asking to go on a date with you. When you have noticed what you are feeling, you've named it, and you've allowed it to be rather than push it away, then you can get back in the driver's seat of your life and choose what you do next. It's all about creating more choices. And it all begins with getting to know your feelings.

TICK THE BOX*

When did you cry last?

I have cried in the last:

Year	☐
Six months	☐
Three months	☐
One month	☐
Week	☐
Day	☐

*If you ticked any of these boxes, you are NORMAL.

ROMY AND BEAR TALK SOME MORE ABOUT FEELINGS

BEAR: Romy, what do I do when Momma and Dadda don't know what I am feeling? They don't understand Googish talk like you do.

ROMY: You can tell me, little brother. How do you feel now?

BEAR: I don't know how I feel. I am learning when it's hungry and when it's tired. It's hard to tell the difference sometimes.

ROMY: I know, little brother. Sometimes I feel angry and then sad, and then I am laughing and crying at the same time. It is very confusing for me too. Like yesterday when I had to leave my friend Peter and I didn't want to. I was so sad and upset but then I didn't want people to see me sad, so I got angry and banged the car seat over and over.

BEAR: And what happened next?

ROMY: I got a crayon and paper and I drew a face of how I felt and showed it to Dadda, and then I felt like I was lighter and I fell asleep.

BEAR: How do you feel now, big brother?

ROMY: I still miss Peter.

WE ARE NOT ROBOTS. WE HAVE FEELINGS. WE HAVE GOT TO FEEL THEM. OTHERWISE, WE ARE ROBOTS. AND WE ARE NOT ROBOTS.

THE FIRST RULE OF FEELINGS . . .

In the movie *Fight Club* there is a set of rules that apply to the members. The first two rules are the same: You Do Not Talk About Fight Club. Feelings used to be the same – you didn't talk about them. You held them close to your beating, breaking heart and screamed on the inside while you pretended to the world that you were all good. Now we talk about our feelings a bit more, but we have a long way to go to make it natural to admit that some days we feel on top of the world and some we feel like the bottom has just fallen out of it! When we learn how to understand our feelings and how to talk about them we realise we are the kings and queens of our kingdoms because we have choice.

The other thing about feelings is that they don't stick around for ever, so don't freak out when you feel one you don't particularly like or that makes you feel uncomfortable. Treat them like friends who you love equally. Don't judge them. Just let them come and go. They are supposed to move. When we get clingy with our feelings, they tend to stick around and rule our lives.

Feel your feelings but don't be their slave. Sometimes we think we have no choice about what we feel. But we do have a choice. Here's the recipe for taking charge of your feelings and not letting them take charge of you:

> Feel them
>
> Let 'em go
>
> Feel them
>
> Let 'em go

It is easy to say, hard to do, but with practice you can feel something and then wave it on. And if a feeling is sticking around and really messing with your head, then go get real professional help. Not everyone has access to a professional, but if you have the opportunity to work with one and there's a chance it might help you, then you'd be crazy not to try it! On the other hand if you like doing things on your own and want to break a feeling wide open and let it pass, try writing about it or drawing it or rapping/singing it, or whatever will allow it to have its day in the sun before moving on. Whenever I get frustrated or feel like a cry would release some energy, I put on the movie *Les Misérables* and wail when the little boy gets shot, and then I'm all good again!

GET TO KNOW WHAT'S GOING ON INSIDE

Because our feelings are often hard to understand but dictate so much of what we get in life, we need a way to navigate them so we are free of their commands. One way to do this is to regularly check in on how your inner universe is rolling.

This is more important than brushing your teeth. So if you have to make a choice between a daily practice of asking yourself what you are feeling or brushing your teeth, then you know the winner! Anyway, if they are the love of your life they will overlook your yellow, about-to-fall-out teeth and still fall for you. So whenever you need to, come back here with a pencil and let it all out. Then erase it and start all over the next time.

CALL TO ACTION

Finish the sentence:

I feel _____
_____
_____
_____

WHAT WE DON'T FEEL, WE FEED

Whatever we don't feel, we feed

Until it becomes a mystery

Why we feel so far from our destiny

So feel it all

Feel every bloody bit of it

The tears, the rage, the love, the loneliness

Come to know them all

As friends

And if you do that, you will never be scared again.

If we don't acknowledge our feelings (and I'm not saying we should wallow in them forever; I'm saying we should honour what we are feeling) they become bigger and hide in the shadows, waiting for an opportunity to get in the driving seat of our lives. They can become bullies that run the show. Befriend them, talk gently to them and sometimes be their momma or poppa and say, "I see you, sadness/anger/disappointment/fill in the blank. I see you and it's all OK. I got this."

MAKE SOME SPACE

Once you've asked yourself what you are feeling and you have some sense of what the hell is going on and why, here are some things to try if you want to make some space inside. Afterwards you can decide what to do next (do you hire an assassin or tell the person how you feel about what they said/did?).

- » Take a twenty-second cold shower (seriously, it works).
- » Dance your head off on your own.
- » Cuddle your pet; tell them how you feel.
- » Write or draw that shit out.
- » Go to the gym and get your heart roaring.
- » Close your eyes and breathe so slowly that people think you've fallen asleep on the bus. Just focus on your breathing.
- » Add your own way that you create space between you and the feelings raging inside you.

_____
_____
_____

Remember, most adults were never taught to (a) understand their feelings or (b) be the ringmaster of their emotional circus, so you may need to teach them how to do it once you've nailed it. And if you need extra help understanding, remember to go see a pro.

ANGER

ANGER

Have you ever wanted to break something, or break someone? I have. We all have. Have you ever wanted to destroy your room just to get the feelings out? I have.

Anger is a beautiful emotion. It is so undervalued. Anger has a power no other feeling has. Because I was angry with the world after my father died, I cycled 7,000 km. Anger is delicious. Anger is your friend when it is expressed properly and directed in a positive direction. Because, like everything in life (especially feelings), anger isn't straightforward. It can also rip you to pieces and create havoc in your heart. It can turn you mean and make you into a monster.

Once I was standing in the middle of a room with 120 fifteen-year-old boys. I asked them a question and told them to stand up if their answer was yes.

I asked, "Who here has ever been so angry about something that you wanted to smash your room to pieces?"

EVERY BOY IN THE ROOM STOOD UP!

Anger is a universal human emotion. Maybe you need to let yourself feel more of it because you feel weaker than you want to, and you want to speak up for yourself more and anger is the match that lights the fuse so you can do that. Or maybe you don't know how to put a leash on your anger and you frighten the people you love when you express it. Maybe once you've put your anger on its leash, you need to take it for a walk to calm it down and show it who's boss.

I want you to know that anger is normal and can be helpful. But it also has a dark side and can get you into situations you will regret and may not be able to put right. So what do you do when you are so full of rage that you would like to set fire to the whole world and watch that fucker burn?

ALLOW THE ANGER AND RAGE TO HAVE THEIR TIME, LET THEM WASH OVER YOU AND THEN TURN THEM INTO SOMETHING POSITIVE. USE THEIR FIRE TO SCORCH A TRAIL TO WHERE YOU WANT TO GO.

TURN ANGER INTO A SUPERPOWER

To turn your anger into a superpower, you need to know how to turn down its volume so you can see what is underneath.

How to turn down the volume on your anger:

1. When you want to smash something and your head is on fire, you need to get it into the cooler box so your next move is a good one. It's time to take three deep breaths as slowly as you can, to allow your brain to kick in.

2. Lie on the ground. Seriously. Did you ever see anyone have a raging argument lying on their back? This will help you calm down enough to know what's really going on.

3. Write, paint, rap, draw your anger and rage on a page. The key is to name the anger and acknowledge what has lit its fuse. This might even mean heading out of the house for a walk just for a change of scenery.

4. If none of that works then jump into a cold shower. It works and it's great for your hair. What you are trying to do is get some distance from the anger you are feeling to understand what's going on underneath.

SEE THE ANGER, FIND THE FEAR

When my friend told me this, it was a lightbulb moment for me. I realised that whenever I've been really angry, underneath the anger I have been afraid of something. Like when I feel like I am being attacked by someone in a conversation and I'm afraid I'll be hurt, or I'm afraid that I'm being rejected or that I'm going to be embarrassed or made look like a fool. Think about it. When you were last really angry, what might have been the fear underneath your anger?

So the next time you're losing it and about to smash the shit out of something, follow steps 1–3 above first, and maybe even the cold shower, too, before the non-smashing part of your brain can kick in. Then ask yourself, "What am I afraid I will lose? What am I afraid is happening? What am I afraid people will think of me? What might be the fear hiding underneath my anger?"

SOMETIMES YOU NEED TO WRECK THAT ROOM TO LEARN THAT'S NOT THE WAY TO SPILL THE FEELING AND FILL THE HOLE INSIDE. THEN ASK YOURSELF - WHAT IS THE FEAR HIDING BEHIND MY ANGER, WHAT AM I AFRAID WILL HAPPEN TO ME?

Chapter 4
FRIENDS

THE MOST BEAUTIFUL SOUND IN THE WORLD IS THE LAUGHTER RISING UP FROM FRIENDS IN A SKATE PARK. FOR THIS TIME THERE ARE NO WORRIES, NO STRESS, NO FEARS - JUST YOU & YOUR MATES & A MILLION THREADS OF A STORY TO BE TOLD.

SOUL TRIBE

Your friends – the real ones – the ones who are your soul tribe will always be there for you. And in life we all need that. Watch out for your friends. Some of them won't be able to talk to their families when they need to. Some won't even have families – you will be that for them.

Cherish these real friends like the air you breathe, because one day they will all be gone.

REAL FRIENDS

When you're around a real friend, you don't feel empty, you don't feel alone and you don't feel like there's something wrong with you. Real friends make you feel you are capable of more than you feel capable of when you're alone. They make you feel bigger inside. Yes they will joke with you and make fun of you, but you know that they would let no one else make fun of you in a mean way. And they'd defend you with their life if anyone tried to hurt you.

Real friends will always be honest with you when you're being an idiot because they know you are better than you can imagine and they want you to be the awesome piece of meteorite dust you came here to be.

Real friends make you feel proud, rather than embarrassed, of your feelings because they have felt the same.

When you are with real friends, you don't have to try to be anyone else, just you, and that's the best thing in the world. Awkward silences, well, they don't exist when you're with real friends. Your most-often used phrase when you're with real mates is, "I was just thinking the same thing . . ."

With real friends, you'll spend hours in the park/at the pitch/on the corner/cruising around and then go home and call them straight away. Your parents won't understand it and will ask, "Were you not with them all day? What could you possibly still have to talk about?" They forget they did the same!

Real friends make you feel brave. With them by your side you feel like you could take on the world because you know they're in your corner.

DURING YOUR LIFE TO COME, WITH REAL FRIENDS YOU WILL:

- » Hold each other when your worlds fall apart (hopefully not at the same time).

- » Hold their hair when they are puking up.

- » Dance at their wedding.

- » Be the person they call when their first child is born.

- » Be there for them when their marriage is falling apart and they are fighting to hold on.

- » Celebrate when they get fired from their job because their boss was an idiot and now they can chase their real dream.

- » Cry with them when they say goodbye to their parents and be there for them as they try and put the shards of their heart back together.

- » Be at each other's kids' biggest days and show the young ones what partying really looks like.

- » Tell the people that have come to say goodbye what your friend was really like and why you loved them, on the day they are sent home to the place we all come from.

THE QUESTION IS ARE YOU A REAL FRIEND?

- Do you encourage your friends to be their unique flavour of weirdness?

- Do you guide them back to their path when they are doing stupid shit or doing stuff just to fit in and be liked?

- Do you ask them how they are when you sense they're not OK? Do you push it when they fob you off because they are embarrassed by how they feel?

YOUR FRIENDS ARE YOUR TRIBE UNTIL YOUR PARENTS HAVE GROWN UP ENOUGH TO SEE YOU AGAIN. SO, MIND EACH OTHER, LOVE ONE ANOTHER'S EXPERIMENTS IN FINDING OUT WHO YOU ARE. THIS IS THE START OF YOUR LIFE AND EVERYTHING IS GOING TO BE OK IN THE END. AND IF IT IS NOT OK, THEN IT IS NOT THE END.

ROMY AND BEAR — PLAYING TIGERS

BEAR: How was school, Romy? I missed you. It seemed like a hundred years waiting for you to come home.

ROMY: It was good, Bear. My friend Iggy was sad today. I saw him sniffling and he had been crying. I don't know why. So I said to him, "Let's play tigers."

BEAR: What's tigers, Romy?

ROMY: It's when we get one of our friends to play the tiger and we chase them in the jungle of the schoolyard. I wanted to make Iggy feel happy, so I did that. It made him forget his sadness. That's what you do for your friends, Bear.

BEAR: I don't have any friends yet, Romy.

ROMY: Of course you do, Bear. You have me. You'll always have me. And I'll always be there for you. And no one will hurt you while I am around, because I have big muscles.

Chapter 5
LIFE

FEAR AND COURAGE

FEAR

Fear can be a real fucker. I won't lie to you; I've had a very troubled relationship with fear. All my life I've been afraid of something. The annoying thing is that the fears have changed shape like slippery chameleons over and over again. Just when I had pierced one and felt it was vanquished, its little brother or sister would pop up, ready to own me all over again. Usually they would come from the same place – the fear that somehow I would fail and be an embarrassment to myself and anyone who ever loved me. That I would let people down and get to the end of my life and realise it had all been a waste. But the story doesn't end there. Over time I've learned to climb onto my fears like they are a wild horse, and rather than destroy them, I've learned to pat the horse's neck and whisper in its ear. I've learned to comfort and ride the horse without breaking its spirit. That's how I've made my fears into my allies.

    I know sometimes you are afraid of things and it annoys you, it frustrates you and makes you feel confused and even weak. I know sometimes you pretend to everyone that you have it all together when in reality you cry yourself to sleep or dream of being old enough to get in a car and drive away so fast from everything that's going on in your life that your fears would never find you. That's OK. That's so bloody normal, I swear to you.

    Fear is one of the most beautiful things us humans can feel. Because our fears are what protect the scared child in us from getting harmed or hurt by the world. When you look at your fears that way – as the cries of the youngest part of you – then you can stop trying to kill your fears and instead bend down and listen to them.

But that doesn't mean that your fears call the shots! No, you are in charge of who does the shooting. In this section I'm going to give you some ways to look at fear and show you what works for me. But don't just use my way – hunt out your own. Because the truth is you will never kill your fears. They are with you like those beautiful eyes of yours and that unique soul-print that only you carry. But you can befriend them and adopt them and make them your allies – your very own wild beast that you ride through the stormy night sky and together you get to the end of your life and the last words you utter are "I did it! I really lived!"

LOVE IS WHAT WE ARE BORN WITH, FEAR IS WHAT WE LEARN

We are born fearing two things: loud noises and falling. Makes sense from an evolutionary perspective, right? Both signal potential death. Apart from those two fears, we are born to receive love and to give it. The rest of our fears we learn.

Over time we develop a personality – a persona, a mask – that we need to develop to survive. This persona helps us to fit in, to receive emotional nourishment just like we received food when we were babies and unable to feed ourselves. About the time our mum, dad or whoever cared for us stopped wiping our bums, this persona took over the job of keeping us safe. It looked around at the family or group you were growing up in and selected a persona that would get you the most acceptance. If that family prized achievement above all else, your persona copped on that this was the path to love and acceptance. If you grew up in a family who lived hard, died young and fought the law, then your persona likely made you tough, showing no vulnerability. That way your tribe accepted you.

But what to do with that vulnerable, childlike part of us we had before we developed a persona? Our persona came up with an ingenious plan. It locked the vulnerable, childlike part of us who cried when they were scared or lonely into an invisible dungeon and nominated a team of sentries to watch over the dungeon and make sure no one ever broke in and harmed this most vulnerable part of us. This kept the harmful world away. This was a pretty good strategy for a while.

But the sentries whose job it is to protect the childlike part of you used fear to control your behaviour so that other people and the world couldn't hurt you. They still use fear to do this today.

Except now you are older and the loyal sentries are limiting your experience of the world. It has become an outdated model of survival. If we want to give and receive love, that means allowing the potential for a certain amount of pain and hurt into our lives. So it's time to relieve the sentries of many of their duties. It's up to us to learn how to do the job of protecting the frightened childlike part of us. Then we can live free of our fears' directives and learn to not be so afraid.

ROMY AND BEAR TALK ABOUT FEAR

BEAR: Romy, every night I hear your footsteps in the hall and then the door to Momma and Dadda's room opens and I see you and my heart leaps with joy. I am in my cot but I watch Dadda pull back the quilt and let you in. Why do you go into their bed each night?

ROMY: Because I wake up in the middle of the night, Bear, and I feel scared.

BEAR: But you're so big. Why would you feel scared?

ROMY: Because I once heard a story about killer clowns and now when I wake up and I am on my own I feel scared that they might be in the dark with a big shiny knife, or maybe hiding in the bathroom, and I feel very afraid. I count 1-2-3 and then I jump out of my bed and run as fast as I can across the hall into Momma and Dadda's bed before the killer clowns can get me.

BEAR: Oh, poor Romy, being afraid. I'm not afraid of those scary clowns. I'm only afraid of when doors bang or when I think Dadda is going to drop me when he is lifting me with only one arm.

ROMY: I used to be afraid of just those two things too, Bear, but then my imagination started telling me I could be hurt by the things it makes up. And it's annoying because the things it's afraid of change all the time. It used to be spiders and then it was scary dolls with massive eyes and now it's killer clowns. And it's weird because once Dadda brought me back to my room and turned on the lights and all the things I thought were in the dark had just disappeared.

BEAR: Where did they go, Romy?

ROMY: I don't know, Bear. They just disappeared. I think they can move faster than light.

BEAR: They must be very fast, like the trees passing the window when Momma and Dadda were driving me home from the hospital.

WHAT ARE YOU AFRAID OF?

As long as our fears are hidden under our beds and in our heads, they will dictate the story of our lives. As soon as we shine a light on them, we are back in the driving seat, ready to follow our soul's plan. We are the masters of our destiny once more.

Over the next few days ask yourself, what are you afraid of? Come back here and list the things you come up with. Examples might be being afraid of what people think of you, or being afraid of hurting others, being taken advantage of, of letting people down, of being alone, of losing your mind, or of making a mistake that you can't put right. It might be that you'll lose people you love or that you'll be laughed at for making a fool of yourself.

CALL TO ACTION

What are your fears?

_____
_____
_____
_____

How do your fears hold you back? (You can do this fear by fear or pick the fear you feel holds you back the most.)

_____
_____
_____
_____

MAKING FEAR YOUR FRIEND

Fear gets a bad name. But all fear is really interested in is keeping you safe. For example, fear says, "Don't be an idiot and jump off a cliff into the sea when you don't know how deep it is." That's a wise fear. Some things you should let someone else do first!

What our fears fear most of all is death. In our earliest years, that meant a fear of physical death. Now the fear is that our persona might die if we feel shame or embarrassment. So our fears do what is intelligent when you see the world from this perspective. They limit how much we express ourselves in the world in case we get hurt. They stop us from asking that person out or chasing that dream or leaving school early against your parents' wishes because you can't wait any longer to do what you really, deeply want to do with your life. These fears, while they have good intentions – to protect us from getting hurt – end up making our worlds smaller and suffocating our possibility.

HOW TO SADDLE UP AND RIDE YOUR FEARS

Step 1 is understanding that while your fears may seem like the enemy, they are actually just stuck in a time warp, thinking you are a vulnerable child who can't take care of yourself. You still may not be able to cook a three-course meal yet (or maybe you are) but you are wise, you have seen a lot and can take care of yourself and that little child inside you too. So practise this mantra to go beyond your fears:

> Dear Fear,
>
> Thank you for looking out for me and protecting me up to now. You've done a bloody good job. But now I am ____

years old and have learned a lot about life. I am wiser now and know how to make sure I survive. So I'm going to take over the role of protecting that vulnerable part of me and you're going to take some well-deserved time off, OK?

With love,

Me.

Step 2: Next you need to listen to your fears. Ask them this: "Why are you afraid of asking that guy out, or of speaking up more, or of not speaking up so much, or of going travelling, or of telling Mam and Dad you want to join the circus?" Just list the things your fears says it's afraid of. (This works for things you are worried about as well, if you're someone who worries a lot.) Get it all out. Write it out on your phone or on a page or draw out the fears. You're looking for FEAR-VOMIT here. Just allowing the fears to be heard is a powerful step in gaining more freedom from them.

Step 3: Once you have all the fears out in the open where you can see them, try this roleplay with the sentry that guards the most vulnerable part of you. (I've used asking someone out as the example.)

You: What's the worst thing that could happen if I ask that guy out?

The sentry standing guard over the most vulnerable part of you: He could say no.

You: And what would be the worst thing about that?

Sentry: Well, he would say no! And the rejection would feel awful.

You: And what would be the worst thing about that if it happened?

Sentry: What? The rejection would feel terrible, and that would make us feel not good enough. He might tell his mates and then everyone would know.

You: And what would be the worst thing about that?

Sentry: Everyone would laugh at us and they might point at us in public and say, "There's the saddo who got turned down."

You: And what would be the worst thing about that?

Sentry: Are you serious? That's a stupid question. It would feel bad. We'd feel hurt. We'd end up single forever and never have someone to go and get ice cream with, and we'd die a dark lonely death on the street, being eaten by some type of animal I've never heard of and no one would come to our funeral and we'd never be remembered and we wouldn't get into heaven.

Now you've worked out the origin of the fear! All fears are like this. When you don't shy away from what your fear feels, it will tell you why it exists. And as you have this conversation with the sentry in charge of all your fears, the fears will lessen because they are being listened to.

This exercise also shows you that not asking a guy out because you're afraid of dying alone is crazy. But fear's job is not to be rational, it's to defend that vulnerable child at all costs and make sure they don't get hurt. Strangely, when we live from our fears (I don't want to end up alone, so I won't ask that guy out in case he says no) we actually end up with the very outcome we feared!

Now you have a choice. And life is better when we have choices. Think of an ice-cream parlour with only one flavour of ice cream, or a clothes shop with only one type of T-shirt in one colour. Pretty boring, right? Now you can soothe your fear's worries by telling it you have a choice in what happens after you ask the guy out. And then you take on the responsibility for taking care of yourself because you know that you can handle whatever comes your way. You are wise and able to cope with a guy saying no to you because that means you are ready for the hundreds of others who are waiting!

HOW TO PARENT YOUR FEARS — A RECAP

1. Understand that the role of your fear is to protect you. Use your mantra.

2. Hear your fear. Hear what it is actually afraid of. Listen as it tells you.

3. Lastly, take the thing it is afraid of and keep asking what's the worst thing that could happen. Let it tell you what it is afraid of at every level of that question. Then ask yourself, "If my fear happened, could I live with the feelings that come with it?" Now you have a choice to be in charge of your fears rather than the other way round.

Now you are in a position to reassure the fear that you are able to handle the consequences of the worst-case scenarios. You have a choice about how you react, and that puts you in control.

I have been doing this for years and it is amazing how brave this process makes you feel. Your fears will no longer pull at your leg, trying to sabotage what could be the life of your dreams.

THE MONSTERS UNDER YOUR BED ARE REALLY IN YOUR HEAD

When you look back on your life, you won't regret what you did half as much as you regret what you didn't do because you were afraid to. So don't let your fears stop you living the life you could if you were braver. There's a part of you that is fearless. You are here to let it all out so the world is a better place because you knew your fears and didn't let them stop your wild heart showing the world that you're here.

COURAGE

How do you get rid of your fears altogether? You don't. You build courage. Each time you say "I'm afraid" but you choose to keep going, you build another fibre of courage. Eventually, if you keep doing the thing that scared you and it doesn't result in your annihilation, you realise that fear is just a warning light, it's not a stop sign.

THE ANTIDOTE TO FEAR IS COURAGE

While the antidote to fear is to build courage, that doesn't mean courage always dominates fear. Courage is shitting yourself with fear but doing it anyway. Courage is when you are really afraid but take your fears and transform them into the most beautiful, daring life that you can live. And courage can be giving into your fears one day but not giving up for good. Courage isn't always a roar, sometimes it's a whisper, through the tears that are streaming off your chin, that says you'll come back tomorrow and try again.

You might have been born into a family where courage means hurting anyone who dares come near you. One of my best friends is called Danny. Danny was stabbed for the first time when he was thirteen. All his life courage was defined by his ability to fight, by how much pain he could inflict on others before they got the chance to do it to him. He was fearless and would back down from no one. But somewhere along the line Danny realised courage is about how much you love. Now, Danny showers everyone he meets with love: the girl in a wheelchair in the playground who smiles from ear to ear when she sees Danny coming because he always makes her laugh, the older man who's longing for touch but is afraid to ask and is disarmed every time Danny gives him a big hug.

Danny learned that real courage lies in opening ourselves up to be hurt, knowing that no one can really hurt us, for deep down we are indestructible. But you might be living in a world where you can be badly hurt if you show love. If that's true for you, I want you to know that it won't always have to be that way. One day you'll take your kid to the park to feed the ducks and you'll look at them and your heart will burst with pride because you chose the courage of love and it was worth it.

CALL TO ACTION

Who's the most courageous person you know and why? Try to be really specific by adding an example of a time you have seen this person show courage.

_____
_____
_____
_____

COURAGE
IS GETTING UP ONE MORE TIME WHEN YOU THINK YOU CAN'T!

ROMY AND BEAR TALK ABOUT COURAGE

BEAR: What's courage, Romy?

ROMY: Courage is when you're afraid but you still do the thing you want to do.

BEAR: I don't understand. How can you be afraid and have the courage thing at the same time?

ROMY: Well, it's like one paints over the other. Or like the traffic lights in town. You know what colour they are, Bear?

BEAR: Yes. They're amber, green and red. I saw them once when Momma was taking me to get my injections, and I always remember them because that was the sorest day ever.

ROMY: Oh, poor little Bear. I hate injections too. So fear is like the amber light. It warns you to be careful and watch out, but then comes green, which is the courage light. It tells you to go for it: "Go on, off you go!" But I heard in playschool last year from my friend James that some grown-ups think fear is the red light.

BEAR: Why do some grown-ups think fear is the red light?

ROMY: Because when they feel afraid, they just stop and they get so stuck where they are that they can't see when the lights turn green, so they just stay where they are and they never get to go to all the cool places that are waiting for them.

BEAR: Grown-ups are very silly, aren't they, Romy? Maybe they need to get more injections to not be so afraid to go even when they're afraid, because then they'd have more fun.

ROMY: I think you're right, Bear. The grown-ups need to go and get the courage injection so they don't get stuck where they are and miss out on all the fun things in life.

57 GUYS

Fifty-seven guys were awkwardly sitting on chairs that scraped the wooden gym floor. They were sitting with their mates in groups spread around the giant room. I didn't know which was worse, the echo or the silence. I decided to take a chance and turn up the heat.

"You guys have been telling me how tough you are in this school, so I want to see it for myself. I'm going to ask you a question, and let's see who has the balls to be honest. Who's the most courageous person in the room? So tell me, what has kept you feeling smaller than you know you are? What have you battled your way through so you could be more of who you want to be?"

There was silence. It sat heavily in the room as the guys looked down at the floor. It got more uncomfortable for them and for me. Guys started breaking their own awkwardness by shouting at their mates to speak up. Just when I was going to call it off, the biggest guy in the room took the floor.

"Fuck it, I'm going for it. When I was a kid, I was fat. I got bullied for it all the way through primary school. A group of kids would wait for me, and whenever I walked in the gate, it started. 'Hey porky, hey fatso, hey chubby cheeks.' As we got older, it got worse and they would tell me I should go to another school because they didn't want fat guys in their school. It was terrible. I acted as if it didn't bother me but it did. Some days on my way to school I would be so nervous I'd vomit. Every day was torture until I found the sport I love. I took all my anger and rage and poured it into that sport. I counted down the days on my wall till I was old enough to leave that place and go to secondary school. Something in me told me that I was OK, that I was going to make it somewhere if I just stuck to my sport. It became the thing I did to escape, to feel good about myself. I kept pouring all the shit I took off those guys into my sport. And now I know that I'm going to go pro, and in a weird way I have a lot to thank those guys for."

"What would you say to them if they were standing here now?" I asked.

"On my own in my bedroom, I used to talk to my reflection in the mirror all the time, practising what I'd say to them. Now I suppose I'd say, 'I know you were just miserable fucks. I know your dad beat you. I know your mother disappeared when you were a baby. I know it was never about me. You guys just were messed up. And thanks – look at me now!'"

He looked around the room. He seemed to be expecting someone to laugh and tried to make sure it wouldn't happen by saying, "I don't care what you guys think of me now, so you can think whatever you want."

Instead, almost as one, the whole group stood up and applauded. They roared. A few of his mates even grabbed their chairs in one hand and raised them high while chanting his name: "Aaron, Aaron!"

Eventually everyone sat down again.

Except one guy.

"My name is Luke, for those in the class that don't know me. I am going through something right now that makes me feel smaller than I know I can be. After listening to that story and seeing how everyone reacted, I want to get something off my chest."

I could feel something significant was about to happen. "Are you sure today is the day?" I asked.

"Yeah, it is. I'm ready."

"OK, go for it."

"I really respect Aaron now. I never dreamed that that was what life was like for him. I only know him as the tough athlete that no one would mess with. You see the thing that keeps me feeling small is that I have a secret. I've always known the thing I keep secret and I'm tired of not being who I want to be. Who I know I am."

"And you're sure you want to let people in on that secret today?" I asked again.

"Yes, so will you just let me?" he shot back.

A voice from the crowd said, "Will you let the guy speak?"

"OK, the floor's yours."

"I hear guys throwing around words like 'gay' and 'faggot' in the corridors and it hurts me and makes me feel scared because what I have always known is that I am gay. That's it, that's the thing that I don't want to hide anymore. I said I'd wait till I got out of school to admit it to the world but I'm done pretending."

He went quiet and his head sank. And then he slowly looked up and faced his classmates with his head held high.

SOMETIMES COURAGE IS DOING THE THING THAT SCARES YOU, ESPECIALLY WHEN YOU DON'T KNOW THE OUTCOME.

The most courageous thing you will ever do is be yourself.

DIRECTION

It can be difficult to decide what to wear on a night out, not to mention what direction to take in life. I once had a cool job. I would go to hospitals and tell doctors about this thing they already knew they needed. It was something cancer patients used when they were having chemo to stop them from picking up infections and dying before they had a chance to recover from the cancer. I got paid well and was given a new car to travel around in. All my friends were jealous because they were working in fast-food joints or other jobs they hated.

One day I realised my heart was telling me to go back to school and follow my real dream. I resisted for a while and told myself that I had everything I needed – a good job, a company car and loads of money. But my heart went from a whisper to a roar. One day I was sitting in my car, about to visit a hospital, when I realised there were tears streaming down my face. When I looked at myself and my tear-stained face and red eyes in the mirror, I had to admit to myself that it was time to follow the road less travelled rather than the safe one I was on.

I found a university on the other side of the world that agreed to take me on an exciting programme, and I told my family. They had their reservations, but when my father told me to go for it, I felt it was the right thing to do.

Then I called my boss. She was a really cool woman and she listened patiently. Then she said, "Let me call you back in a half hour." When she called back, she told me that if I stayed the company would give me a BMW and, in time, more money. I was twenty-one and I was being offered a dream car and more money to do a job I found very easy. It was a dilemma. My head wanted one thing and my heart wanted another.

Later that day, I bumped into a guy who had done the same job that I was doing all his life and was nearing retirement. I confided in him about how I was conflicted. He put me straight. He told me that his one regret was that he hadn't followed his dream. Yes, he had a nice house and had put his kids through university. Yes, he went on two holidays a year and his lawns were the nicest in the area. But the other reality was that some nights he lay awake at night and asked himself what his life would have been like if he followed what it was he really wanted to do when he was a younger man. A few weeks later I left everything that was safe and secure and set out to find the life I hoped was waiting for me.

I've never regretted it.

THE DNA OF DIRECTION

You will get lost.

Your dreams will get derailed.

That's the way it's supposed to be.

But don't worry.

When you get to where you were always meant to be, you will have the whole world inside you.

And the universe at your fingertips.

CHOOSING A DIRECTION

Don't do what your parents tell you to. They want you to be safe and have a steady job. There's no such thing as a steady job anymore. Don't listen to your parents unless they are telling you to trust yourself and follow your heart.*

This is life and death, man. So don't take advice from anyone who says, "This is just the way the world works." They are already dead and trying to cling to a certainty that may keep you safe but also keeps you small on the inside.

---

* *If you are acting the idiot and doing really stupid stuff and your parents are kind people and are saying, "You're better than this," then this is the exception to the rule, and you should listen to them, especially if they did stupid shit themselves once and regretted it.*

ROMY AND BEAR TALK ABOUT DIRECTION

BEAR: Romy, why do grown-ups get so lost when they get big?

ROMY: Because they forget the plan they made before they got big.

BEAR: How do they forget?

ROMY: Well, they go to a place called a school that fills their heads so full of lots of things that they forget who they are and how to listen to their hearts. These school places are very good at making you believe you're only a head.

BEAR: But, Romy, if they forget to listen to their hearts, they won't be able to follow their soul's plan. That is not good. That's worse than if I lost my blankie and didn't know how to ever find it again. How do they know what to do if they don't know how to listen to their heart or follow their soul?

ROMY: They don't! They listen to other grown-ups who say they should do this or do that, and they look in all the wrong places for answers about what to do and where to go. Bit by bit they can even get sick because they are so confused.

BEAR: That's just poopy, Romy. I never want to go to one of those school places or to be a grown-up.

ROMY: But, Bear, even if we forget our soul's plan when we grow up, it's never too late to remember. Because our hearts never stop whispering to us. And don't worry – I'll make sure you never forget how to listen to your heart, because I love you more than you love your blankie.

BEAR: Wow, you really do love me, Romy. I'm a lucky little brother to have you as my school.

DON'T BE A SLAVE

Slavery was abolished because it steals our soul's freedom to self-direct towards our purpose on earth, which is to remember who we really are. Choosing a career based on what you think you should do, rather than what you would love to do, is also a form of slavery because you are not in charge of the direction of this precious life you are living.

When you choose your career in life you could be unknowingly handing yourself over to a life in which you feel like you are caged with no way out. This is why: If you choose "a safe career path" that usually means safe from a financial point of view. The advantage of a safe job is that you will be able to earn money on a consistent basis for the rest of your life. Where does this get you? You get a house with a mortgage, which is a loan that you pay back over a long period of time and if you fail to pay the loan, the bank can take your house. Your parents might encourage you to get a safe, solid job. The flaw in that approach is that **there is no such thing as a safe, solid job anymore.**

If you get the safe, solid job and a mortgage, you are tied up before you have learned what you want to do with your life. When you begin with safe, steady and well paid as the deciding factors in your choice of career, you are taking part in the building of your own cage. Do whatever you wish, but just remember that if you start with "How do I help other people?" and then move on to "and I want to earn a good living," you will always find purpose in what you do. And if you are helping others and doing what you really enjoy, the money has an amazing habit of showing up anyway, even though you didn't start out with money as your primary motivation. This is the road to happiness.

FLAWS IN THE SAFE-SOLID-JOB APPROACH

1. It doesn't necessarily teach you about who you are.
2. It is built on an economic model that has been shown to be fundamentally flawed and extremely fragile.
3. You are far too wise to choose a career path for your entire life unless it is such a strong calling it pulls you in the direction your heart and soul wants to go.

Most of the jobs school is preparing you for will not exist in ten years' time.

Your parents want security and safety for you. But when they say they want that for you, they're not thinking of you; they're thinking about the security. And they're not necessarily happy with where they are, with the job they're in, so they're not really qualified to give you advice. Tell them that. And then tell them to come see me if they are not happy with it. That doesn't mean you can stay in bed all day, eat their food, use their car, spend their money and have no direction or not fight for the life you could be living. If you say you'll do it your way, then you win the top prize, which is to be the one in charge of what happens next. You are the captain of your life.

Jobs come and go.

Careers change.

Money will not make you happy.

So if you make it your main goal in life, prepare for disappointment.

TRUST YOURSELF!

YOU ARE WISER THAN YOU REALISE.

IN THE END IT'S UP TO YOU

If you don't like what you are getting, you'll have to change, or everything is going to stay the same.

Change on the inside and things will change on the outside.

Don't blame anyone else if you are not where you want to be.

That's a waste of energy.

The bottom line is you can change where you are but only after you stop trying to change everyone else.

Look in the mirror and get to work on changing yourself from the inside out.

If you follow your dreams, it will demand some discipline. You will have to get up early, stay late, go in when you don't feel like it, try again when you feel like giving up.

But if you are on the path to your dreams, your parents won't have to tell you to get up, because your heart will do that for you.

So find the direction that pulls you along. Then it will be much easier to go hunting when you don't feel like you have it in you today!

PERMISSION

Whatever direction you take, don't wait for other people's permission to live an extraordinary life, no matter who they are, and no matter how much you deserve their blessing. Don't wait for it. Try with everything you have not to need their approval before you begin. The ones who really love you and see you for who you are will be in your corner. Cherish those people – they are keepers.

Chapter 6
HARD TIMES

ROMY AND BEAR TALK ABOUT HARD TIMES

ROMY: Bear, do you know what to do when everything falls apart?

BEAR: No, I don't, big brother.

ROMY: First, Bear, there is something you need to know about me.

BEAR: What is it, Romy?

ROMY: I love Lego. I love it so much. Sometimes it is all I can think about, and when I can't sleep, Dadda tells me to think about my favourite Lego, and I do that till I fall asleep. My favourite Lego is Harry Potter Lego, because I love Harry Potter. One time I got this really cool Lego set – the Weasleys' house from Harry Potter – and I was showing it to someone and it fell and broke into pieces. It had taken me two days in my room to build and now it was in hundreds of pieces on the carpet.

BEAR: Were you sad?

ROMY: I was never so sad about anything ever. I cried till my head was sore. I had to start all over again and it took me two days, which I think is like a year in grown-up time. Do you know what I learned, Bear? I learned that life is not fair and things fall apart sometimes, and after you have cried and got angry and banged your bedroom door, there is only one thing to do.

BEAR: What do I do when that happens to me and my toys break and it feels like everything has fallen apart?

ROMY: You start again with just the next thing you can do. No matter how small it is, you ask yourself, "What's the next thing I can do?" And then you keep adding the next piece until you've built the Lego set all over again. It's hard, but once you keep adding the next piece, you'll get there.

BEAR: Romy, can I see the Lego you built after it broke and you had to rebuild it next piece after next piece?

HARD TIMES

If you relate to anything in the list below because you or someone you know has lived through/are living through them, I want you to put your hand in the air (even if you are reading this on the bus or in the park! You can pretend you are saying hi to a friend if you're afraid people will think you are crazy!)

Bullying

Depression

Anxiety

Sexuality

Alcohol problems

Parents divorcing

Lost friends

Did something you regret

Felt your family were disappointed in you

Family member died

Suicidal thoughts

Suicide attempts

Panic attacks

Self-harm

Worrying about friends who are suicidal

Loss of self-confidence

Sexual abuse

Criminal conviction

Family separation

Had your heart broken

I wish I could say life is going to be one smooth ride all the way to the finish line and that a marching band will guide you to the winners' enclosure. But whether or not you raised your hand because you have lived through something in the list, the reality is that hard times come to us all. Some of you reading this have already experienced things that have shown you that life can be cruel. People can hurt you, and bad things happen to good people.

If you are reading this and thinking, *I've had a great life and only good things are on my horizon,* then I have something to tell you that deep down you already know:

LIFE WILL BREAK YOUR HEART.

Ask any person near the end of their life and they'll tell you there were some glorious moments and some moments that even decades later hurt so much that late at night they weep like they're happening all over again. One dear friend of mine still wakes up in the middle of the night and talks to his wife who died years ago and cries because he misses her lying beside him. Life knocks the edges off all of us so the way to our hearts is smoother.

Whatever happens in your life, don't let it close the shutters of your heart. No matter what terrible things have happened to you, it isn't your fault. But it is your call what happens next.

So what I want to offer you is a way to get through to the other side when something extraordinarily difficult hits you. I mean a way to move through a major life challenge like the death of a friend, a divorce that shows you the worst side of your parents, getting an illness that scares you – that level of shit is what I am talking about. The three strategies outlined below come from Dr Lucy Hone, a resilience researcher who had to put her training to personal use when her twelve-year-old daughter and her friends were killed in a tragic car accident. These three ways of thinking will help you find your way through and grow your resilient, defiant, wise soul.

1. BAD SHIT HAPPENS

We don't want bad things to happen but one way to navigate the hard time you are going through is to realise that just because you are you doesn't mean bad shit won't happen to you. Bad shit happens to all of us, and that includes even you! Suffering is part of being human. Accepting that bad shit happens in life will help you avoid taking up permanent residency in the country called "Why me?", also known as "Why has this happened to me?", "Life is so unfair" and "Why does bad shit always happen to me?"

The truth is, why not you? You're human, right? Sadly, hard times are part of being human. Period. No matter what you are going through, after you've cried those painful tears, tell yourself, "Bad shit happens to everyone in life and that's just the way it is." Perfect lives don't exist, and if you see someone on Instagram whose life looks perfect, they've tricked you into believing what they want the world to believe.

2. HUNT FOR THE GOOD STUFF

Our brain has three times the space dedicated to seeing threats and dangers than to seeing the good stuff. So we have to hunt for the good stuff. I'm not saying that you should deny that things are hard and bad stuff is going on; I'm saying tune in to the good that's happening. You do this in two stages.

First, find the things you can change and accept the things that you can't control or change. Like when my father died, at a certain point I just had to accept I couldn't change it, but I could change the way I was living with it. So I focused on living a life he would love to see me living, because I knew he was watching.

Once you've decided on what you can change, the next part is to hunt for the good stuff. Here you shift your attention to find the good things that are happening. This is a skill and you will get better at it with practice. Try this: every night when you are going to sleep ask yourself, "What were three good things that happened today?" Over time you may start to feel better about life and hopefully you'll look forward to lying in bed and going back over the movie of a day in your life and picking your three favourite scenes. I do this with my son a lot and we love it. You can even do it at any time during the day. Try it right now for yourself.

3. ASK YOURSELF IF WHAT YOU'RE DOING IS HELPING YOU OR HARMING YOU

This question is so powerful it's like a rocket booster. If you're going through a hard time and you are piecing your life and your sanity back together, this question is your best friend. You can ask it about anything when you are trying to get somewhere in life, but it's particularly good when you're finding your way through a painful time when each day feels like crawling through the worst moments imaginable.

» Is the way you are thinking or acting helping you or harming you?

» Is what you are about to do (kiss your best mate's girlfriend, for example) going to help you, or is it going to harm you?

» Is stalking your ex on Insta helping or harming you? It may even be helping you (because it's making you realise what an idiot they are and that you are better off without them), but it might be harming you. The great thing about this question is it works as a shortcut to determining what is and isn't working for YOU!

Asking the help/harm question gives you back some sense of

control because it puts you in charge of the next move. It can help to determine how long the feelings associated with the hard time stay and how painful they are.

Thanks to Dr Lucy Hone for her permission to present "The Three Secrets of Resilient People" where she shares the above three strategies to get through hard times.

Go have a look at her Ted Talk if you want to hear an incredibly brave woman tell her story and give more detail on these strategies.
See Lucy's Ted Talk at https://www.ted.com/talks/lucy_hone_3_secrets_of_resilient_people?language=en

WHEN LIFE DOES KNOCK YOU DOWN JUST KNOW THAT YOU HAVE IT INSIDE YOU TO GET BACK UP AGAIN, AND AGAIN, AND AGAIN.

THE OTHER SIDE OF HARD

The best experiences in life are on the other side of HARD.

So don't:

Give up

Make an excuse for why not to try one more time

Complain so much that you are that person everyone finds a pain to be around

Doubt yourself

Give others who are trying to do something you don't understand a hard time

And don't lose faith

And remember, at our lowest points things can happen that some would call miracles. I can't explain it but I've seen it again and again. Most people don't know when miracles are happening because they've stopped believing they are even possible.

HEY, COTTON-WOOL KID

There is an opinion out there that the teenagers of today are soft. What that means is that you lack grit, determination and the ability to bounce back from hard knocks that your parents and other generations had. The thinking is that your parents received very little expressed love from their parents, and their parents received even less from their parents, and so on (stiff upper lips were needed to endure famines, revolutions, civil wars, ethnic cleansings, world wars, cold wars and dogmatic religions that all but outlawed tenderness). Whatever the reasons, it is said that your parents have been too soft on you and gave you everything they didn't get, especially lots of cuddly love. And then a culture of "everything now" did the rest to turn you into overweight, lazy, brittle little darlings who act like the world will take care of you.

I DON'T BUY IT.

The truth is we've all been softened by the ease of the immediate-takeaway, everything-at-your-fingertips world, the grown-ups as well! They're just as addicted to their phones as you are.

I have met thousands of teenagers who, once they've found their thing, work their asses off and fight like hell to do more of the thing they love. And the truth is that life is going to throw hard times at you because that's what your soul wants so it can expand and remember who it is. A life with challenges along the way is your soul's version of a hard training session. It hurts at the time but it makes you stronger. Your parents can't protect you from that. It's the law of the universe that you will get knocked down by life and be asked to get back up.

So when your parents say, "Ah, in my day...", tell them to go and jump in the sea. And remind them that yours is the generation that's going to clean up the mess they and all the generations before them have made of the world because they didn't know any better. And you do, and you're going to put it right, right?

WITHOUT PAIN WE WOULD LEARN NOTHING. AND IF WE LEARN NOTHING, THEN WE HAVE MISSED THE POINT OF THIS ADVENTURE CALLED BEING ALIVE.

ROMY AND BEAR TALK ABOUT PAIN

ROMY: Bear, I want to tell you about pain.

BEAR: Like that time I hit my face on Dadda's shoulder, that pain?

ROMY: Yes, like that time. But there are so many ways we can feel pain, little brother. You felt ouch pain in your body that time. But there's also ouch pain in your heart when something hurts your heart.

BEAR: I don't know that type of pain. Do you get it when you hit your heart off something?

ROMY: No, it's the opposite to ouch pain in your body. It's not when you hit your heart off something, it's when something invisible touches your heart. Something happens and it sends a pointy arrow to your heart and your heart goes ouch, and it really, really hurts.

BEAR: I'm frightened of that arrow hitting my heart and how that will feel. Has it happened to you, Romy?

ROMY: Yes, one time Dadda gave out to me because a boy said I hit him, but the truth was that the other boy was trying to kill a ladybird and I love ladybirds, so I pushed him away and he hit me in the face and then ran and told all the grown-ups that I hit him. Dadda believed him and not me and I felt the pointy arrow hit my heart and the ouch pain in my heart really hurt.

BEAR: I'm feeling the pain in my heart now, Romy. It's because I feel sad for you that that happened.

ROMY: It's OK to get ouch pains in your heart, little brother. Because if we didn't feel the ouches, we wouldn't be able to feel the good feelings in our heart. Will I tell you what to do when your heart gets hurt?

BEAR: Yes, please, Romy, because it feels so heavy in my heart right now and I want it to go away.

ROMY: I will teach you, my cute little Bear. When you get a pointy arrow to the heart and it's really, really sore, you have to let the pain out. You have got to say hello to the pain feeling and tell it you will take care of it, and how you do that is you say to it, "I am going to cry until your pain is gone and then I am going to cry some more." And that's it. It's that simple. You cry till you have no tears left and your heart will say to you, "Thank you. Now I can breathe again."

The sad thing is that grown-ups are so scared that people will make fun of them that they've forgotten how to help their hearts breathe. Some of them even pretend that they don't feel when their heart gets hurt. When they don't allow themselves to feel their heart, eventually they get so sad that you can see it in their eyes and they can't see the blue sky anymore. But not us, Bear, we know what to do.

BEAR: Yes, Romy, we do. And you're the wisest big brother ever. I hope we are always close to each other and I never lose you, because if I did then I wouldn't have enough tears to cry to help my heart breathe again.

ROMY: Don't worry, Bear. We're blood brothers till the end and we will never forget how to take care of our hearts and help them breathe when they get hurt.

PAIN AND HEALING

There are many types of pain. There's the physical type when you stub your toe on a door or stand on a nail or, my personal favourite, walk into a glass door (seriously, I did that once). These all hurt. But there is something about emotional pain, or psychic pain, that can knock us over. You know the type – the type we feel when we hear someone we thought was a friend talk shit about us behind our back, or like when a parent judges you even if they don't come out and say it, or you lose someone you love or something you love, like a pet you have had all your life, and you can't make sense of it.

Once, a girl I loved was in a band. Every summer her band would travel to play in competitions. I was working in a factory doing possibly the most boring job imaginable. All I did all day was put a piece of metal in a machine, close the door, press the green button, let the machine do its thing and then open the door, take out the piece of metal and repeat the process. If you think that was boring to read, imagine doing it for eight hours a day, many days with a hangover!

One day I wanted to chat to my girlfriend as I hated my job so much it really made me miss her. She was away with her band, so I had to wait for her to call me. A few days later she called and she was different. I knew something was up. Then she told me that she had kissed one of the other guys in the band and didn't know how she felt about me anymore. I didn't know it at the time but that was the beginning of the end of us. I told her it was OK and hung up and cycled back for the afternoon shift at the factory. All afternoon and for days afterwards I just stared into the machine and was glad that we had to wear face masks because my eyes kept filling with tears. I was embarrassed to tell anyone what had happened. I just buried it. All the while I felt something I had never felt before. It was a pain I didn't recognise. It felt like nothing I had ever experienced and I hated the feeling. I didn't know what to do to make the pain go away, so I said to myself, "Dry your fucking eyes, stop your sniffling and get over her."

I tried. But I loved her and so it took a long time before the feeling went away.

I know that you have felt that kind of pain. And I know that sometimes the adults in your life don't give your pain the respect it deserves. They think things don't hurt when you're fifteen or sixteen, that it can't be as painful as when something knocks their heart sideways. They don't always understand that someone your age could feel such pain when you've been cheated on, or someone doesn't like you as much as you like them. Or they fail to see that the reason you don't want to leave your room is because you don't think you can face the world. It's not their fault that they underestimate your pain. They've just forgotten how much you can feel when you are your age.

Your parents felt pain when they were your age too. They still do. And they either don't tell you about it because they don't want to appear like they don't have their shit together, or they don't remember how it felt because they've buried it so deep that all it does now is tug at them in the middle of the night. It might not get room during the day, but that only means it shouts louder when it's dark and they're alone with themselves.

I wish I could stop pain from reaching your heart. I wish I could tell you it's never going to hurt, that life will always feel good. But then again, you already know that's impossible, because you are a wise soul.

But can I offer you this:

PAIN IS JUST THE WAY YOUR HEART GETS BROKEN WIDE OPEN SO THAT IT CAN GROW BACK STRONGER THAN IT WAS BEFORE.

When you understand pain and know that it won't last forever, and if you don't let it burn away your hope, you will grow like never before. You will understand the pain of others and proudly show the scars you picked up along the way. Other people will look into your eyes and know you have felt the pain of heartbreak. They will trust you enough to tell you about the shape of their pain and they will shed tears with you because they know you understand and will not judge them.

So don't be afraid of pain. It can heal you so that you can help others do the same.

HOW TO GET THROUGH A PAIN TUNNEL

1. Cry the tears that are needed to wash away the pain. Take Romy's advice to Bear and cry till there are no more tears and then cry some more. I wish I had done that when a girl broke my heart. Cry your tears in private if you need to, or if you have a mate who you know won't judge you, tell them you need them, call around, make sure their parents are out and cry them an ocean.

2. Talk to someone you love and who you know will understand. If they're a real friend, they'll understand, and if they don't or if they make you feel strange, then they aren't the sort of friend you'll keep with you till you both say bye-bye and get your wings!

3. If the pain won't go away after you've cried it out and talked it out, you might need to talk to a professional. Nothing should get in the way of you going after your dreams and living the best life you can, so don't let a painful experience be the thief of your future.

PAIN MAKES YOU STRONGER

Most people run from pain. So do I. But on the occasions when I've run headlong into it, I've felt more alive, wiser, stronger, bigger, more full of love than before. So don't be afraid of pain, because it comes with a gift inside. It's part of life and you better get used to it. Pain and Potential come through the same door. The more you love the more you open yourself to pain. But life is too short to shut the door on love because you're afraid of getting hurt.

Think about it like this: fast food tastes great while you're eating it, but soon afterwards you feel like shit. But with pain, when you're experiencing it, it feels like shit. But afterwards it will leave you feeling bigger on the inside, because you know you came through the storm. Now you can live even braver than before.

Lick your wounds, care for them, learn the lesson, and come back stronger.

WHEN PAIN COMES YOUR WAY VICTIMS SAY, WHY ME? HEROES SAY, LET'S SEE.

LET'S SEE WHERE THIS PAIN CAN TAKE ME, WHAT IT CAN HELP ME BE.

YOU'RE NOT ALONE

I once almost stepped in front of a bus on Coburg Road because I couldn't take it anymore and wanted to leave. Now I watch my son running across a newly cut grass field with his blondie-brown hair blowing like a cape behind him and I thank whatever angel reached down and made me step back onto the pavement.

Oh, sweet angel, thank you. Thank you for what you knew I would miss if I left.

Sometimes the pain we feel is great and we don't know why it hurts so much. Maybe we understand where it is coming from, maybe we don't. Either way, it's still painful. Sometimes we want it to just stop. When that happens, there's only one way out and that is through. But you don't have to travel alone. You're not meant to. So don't. And don't leave. There are moments waiting for you, like beautiful children running across golden fields. And there's an angel who wants to help you get there.

FIGHT

Life is going to challenge you again and again and again. Just when things are going great, something can happen that knocks you out. You will get hurt. The people you love will get hurt. They will die. Unfair things will happen. People will disappoint you and let you down. Shit will happen.

So, you have to find your fight. That way, when you need it, you can tap into it. This is the part of you that regardless of whether you're big or small, skinny or large, Black or white, gay or straight, human or zombie knows that when you need to you can fight for what you believe in and never give up.

Sometimes no one will be able to help you. The cavalry won't always come to save you. Sometimes in life no one can take your place and go into the dark forest and fight your dragons for you. It's your path into the forest and it's your dragon, and whether you go and look for it or it comes and taps its tail on your shoulder, the dragon is yours to fight.

Fight doesn't mean punching someone's teeth out at 2.30 a.m. on the street because they insulted you, or you have taken something and feel invincible. That's just being an idiot.

What I mean about finding your fight is this: Nothing will hit you as hard and try to keep you down as much as life. So don't blame anyone else when this happens. This won't fix it. This won't make the dragon go back where it came from. Sometimes you have to face up to the scariest thing – whether it's coming out, telling that bully to fuck off or saying no to a path that's going to get you killed or put away. It's fighting for who you want to be no matter who around you or what voice inside you says you're not going to make it, that good things like that never happen to people like you, that some things are too good to come true.

Don't let them take your fight away. Whatever comes your way, hold on to your fight. Don't be a coward and hurt others because you think it makes you safer. That won't help you feel good about yourself. Maybe for a moment you'll feel less alone in the pain you're feeling but in the long run it will create a hole in your heart so big that not even a transplant will save you.

SO WHEN THE DRAGON COMES FROM THE DARK FOREST INTO YOUR LIFE, FIND YOUR FIGHT...

BECAUSE NO MATTER HOW YOU DOUBT YOURSELF – YOU HAVE IT IN YOU.

Fight with everything you've got.

Fight for your life like you are willing to die if that's what it takes.

Fight unfair, demeaning, small-minded, racist, hateful people with a love for your own life so fierce that they have no choice but to move out of your way and bow their heads because they are in the presence of a god.

Chapter 7
LOVE

ROMY AND BEAR TALK ABOUT LOVE

BEAR: Romy, what is love?

ROMY: Love is life, Bear. Love is the way to life.

BEAR: I don't think I understand.

ROMY: OK, let me explain it this way, my little bro. When you were in Momma's belly a few months ago, what did you feel?

BEAR: I felt safe. And then I learned Momma's voice and sometimes when it was just me and her and there was no one else around, she would rub me and talk to me and I felt like there was nothing else in the world. Just us. And I just felt cosy and warm and nice.

ROMY: That was love, Bear.

BEAR: Have you felt the love thing, Romy?

ROMY: Of course, Bear. I feel it every time I am with you. I'm feeling it right now. What I have learned is that there is one BIG LOVE and a lot of different loves that are like little streams flowing out of the same big river.

BEAR: Wow! I want to know all about the big river and all the little streams, Romy.

ROMY: Will I tell you the stream we are in right now, Bear?

BEAR: Yes, yes, please tell me.

ROMY: We are in the brother-love stream, except how I feel about you, Bear, is more like a massive waterfall, like the biggest ever waterfall you can imagine. That is how much love I have for you, Bear.

BEAR: Me too, Romy. I'm so happy to have a big brother like you who knows all about the big love and the little streams.

Love is the only thing in the world that can break your heart and also put its broken pieces back together again.

All love comes from the same place, from remembering that we are all really pieces of the magic meteorite dust that landed on earth. I am not going to tell you how to love. I'm still learning, so I don't have enough to say. And sometimes I still forget how to love and how to accept love. But I want to share with you what I have learned about love:

LOVE IS THE MOST POWERFUL WEAPON ON EARTH.

Love can and will fill you up when all else is lost and you think you want to die. Love is the one thing that can fill the hole inside your heart. When we go back to the place we all came from, the only thing you'll have is how much love you left behind. Added up, all the love we leave behind will fill every black hole in the universe.

WE ARE HERE TO REMEMBER HOW TO LOVE

THE MORE YOU ACCEPT AND LOVE YOURSELF THE MORE YOU HELP OTHERS TO DO THE SAME. AND THAT IS THE GREATEST ACHIEVEMENT EVER - THE REASON WE WERE BORN. AND IT ALL STARTS WITH YOU GIVING THE MIRROR A KISS ONCE IN A WHILE.

LOVE YOURSELF

Love moves in two ways: we give love and we receive love. And it all begins with remembering . . .

You are worthy of love because you were born. You are no accident. You are meant to be here. You are worthy of love because you are breathing and your heart is pumping and your soul is beating. You are worthy of love and so is everyone you have ever met. Even the murderers, bombers, rapists, liars and especially the ones on their phone texting in their car at the traffic lights as they turn from green to red while you are waiting behind them shouting for them to move. They are the ones that deserve the most love of all!

RECEIVING LOVE

I used to not like myself. I used to really think the person looking back at me in the mirror wasn't worthy of love. Every lunchtime during school my friends and I would walk up the town to hang out, and every day we'd walk past a jeweller's shop. I hated that jeweller's shop and dreaded walking by it. It had this mirror that you could see yourself in from fifty metres down the street. As you got closer you could see a 3D image of yourself. Don't ask me how it worked; I haven't a clue. What I do know is it made me feel shit because it exaggerated the two things I hated about myself. First, it made me look skinnier than I was – and that was hard to do! My friends loved taking the piss out of how skinny I was, so I didn't need a mirror to exaggerate it even more.

Then as we got closer the mirror showcased the other thing I really disliked about myself – my big crooked nose. I would look anywhere but in that mirror. I hated how that image that greeted me every day at lunch made me feel. Yeah, yeah, I know, I could have crossed the street, but then I would have felt even more defeated.

I wanted to feel different because I was on the way to meet my first love. She was beautiful, and we had known each other since we were kids. When her friends asked me if I would go out with her, I thought it was a prank. Why would this beautiful girl want to go out with me? Well, miracle of miracles, she did! Every day we'd meet at lunch and go to a car park and stand against a wall by a river. We would talk and sometimes kiss and both hope we wouldn't meet one of our parents on their way to the shops. Especially because her dad wasn't my biggest fan! I suppose the earring didn't make me the ideal boyfriend for his daughter, or maybe it was the nose ☺

When I look back now, I wish I could take that sixteen-year-old for a walk around the corner and give him this talk:

> You are a hot bit of sixteen-year-old meteorite dust that has just happened to land in this town.
> Yes, you are skinny.
> Yes, you have a big nose.
> And, yes, it's crooked.
> But get over it!
> You see that girl there, wondering why a grown man has taken her boyfriend around the corner? You are her first love. And she loves you for YOU, not for the shape of your body or the size of your nose or the size of anything else for that matter!
> She loves you for those sparkling blue eyes and smiley face and how you make her feel by just being you, so don't waste this unbelievable opportunity to date the best-looking girl in town by stressing that you are not good-looking enough for her. Stop being an idiot and focus on what you have and accept that one day you'll love the bits you hate right now.
> Now go back around the corner and grab her in your arms and kiss her so hard that you both might fall into that river and then you'll have to save her and so you will be a hero as well as a damn good kisser.

I know there are parts of you, and maybe all of you, that you don't like or accept right now. I'm not going to tell you to get over it. Most adults feel the same way as you and don't like or accept parts of who they are. All I want you to know is that you are enough. You are more beautiful or handsome than you realise right now.

One day you'll feel really comfortable in your skin. One day you'll look at that big nose or the big ass you think you have or the puny chest or the too-curly hair or too-straight hair or the crooked teeth or bad skin or whatever you don't like about yourself and you will actually love it because you have learned to think, *Fuck yeah, this is part of me and I like being me.*

It's important to know that you have a say in how you feel about yourself. We are going to look at that in a while.

And the most important thing of all is on the next page.

MIRROR SISTERS

Once, I found myself in a tiny bathroom with four women in their forties. We ended up there because we had been talking about how hard it can be to fully accept yourself and see yourself as beautiful. How hard it can be to love yourself. So we said we'd try something. We all squashed into the bathroom, faced the mirror and agreed that at the exact same time we'd all say "I love you" to our reflection. We counted down 3-2-1. And there was silence. We couldn't do it. We were all too afraid of what the others would think, and two of the girls said they couldn't say it if they didn't believe it. Eventually, after several attempts, we were able to say, "I want to love you." That was the best we could do. Why is it we can love others but sometimes find it hard to accept and love ourselves?

Did you ever hear someone say, "She loves herself, that one!"?

What they're actually saying is that they wish they could feel the way that girl seems to. In truth, when you love yourself, you don't make others feel inferior. Feelings of inferiority are never about someone else. It's all about how we feel about ourselves.

I can't talk Googish like Romy, so I can't communicate with babies. But if I did I would love to ask a newborn baby, "Do you love yourself?" Do you ever look at yourself in the mirror when you're being changed and you say to yourself: "Look at your double chin, and those chubby cheeks, and, oh my God, your ass looks so big in that nappy. You really do have a funny-looking forehead, and as for your hair – you bald little thing, you – like, really, would you try harder to grow a bit of hair to hide that big forehead of yours?"

Or maybe it's more their behaviour babies would rip into. Like do they say, "You really didn't coo sweetly enough there. Do you want your mother to think you don't like her? Come on, you could have done better."

No. I don't think babies give themselves a hard time like many teenagers and adults do.

Do you give yourself a hard time? Do you have an internal critical voice that points out your inadequacies and imperfections, that reminds you of when you said something stupid, or looked like an idiot on a night out, or that comments on what you're wearing? Is that the voice of someone you'd like to hang out with if it lived outside you?

The truth is that this inner critical voice is something all human beings share. Some people say you just need to think positively and repeat affirmations and it will go away. Being positive and repeating affirmations can help, but I don't think they're the full answer. Other people say just ignore it and tell this negative voice to leave you alone. I think that only makes it grow louder. So how do you make the voice a friendly one and not one that robs your life of joy? How do you quieten its attacks so that you can fully accept yourself?

WHY WE FALL OUT OF LOVE WITH OURSELVES, AND HOW WE CAN FALL BACK IN

Unlike the sentries we met earlier, who use fear to alert you to how you could get hurt by the world around you, your inner critical voice focuses on your own behaviour and appearance to make sure you don't do or say anything that will make others hurt you.

This voice came to our aid early in our lives. It has been with us since we were small children. It learned to keep you safe from being given out to or made to feel pain or shame by criticising you before your parents, or anyone else for that matter, could.

The thing is, over time this voice took one too many steroids and got bigger. Over time it became obsessed with its job of protecting you from being shamed or hurt. All it wants is for you to be OK. It's like that annoying friend who keeps telling you that you can't do this or can't do that, that this or that is dangerous. Basically, it's afraid of the world and wants to protect you. Except it doesn't know when to stop. And it grows until it undermines you and makes your life hard because it constantly, silently tells you when you don't measure up.

What does your inner critical voice tell you is wrong with you? What is not good enough about how you look, act or operate? What are its top three things?

Mine are:

1. You're not working hard enough.
2. You need to go to the gym more. You're getting love handles.
3. Why aren't you having as great a life and being as adventurous as the people you follow on Instagram?

What are yours?

1. _____
2. _____
3. _____

FALLING BACK IN LOVE WITH OURSELVES

As we now know, your inner critical voice has a similar job to the sentries who protect you from getting hurt and dying by using fear to control your behaviour. So how we fall back in love with ourselves is by recognising that every one of the voice's comments are an attempt to protect us. And the way back to ourselves is to discover what lies underneath the critical voice's fears.

When you hear yourself saying or thinking something negative about yourself, ask the thought:

- » What are you afraid of?
- » What are you scared of?
- » What are you trying to protect me from?

Then you can reassure this inner critic that you are big and brave enough to handle its fears of what will happen if you be yourself more of the time. The more you are yourself, the better you will feel and the more you will begin to fall back in love with yourself.

WHAT WILL THEY THINK?

This is one of the main things, if not *the* main thing, that holds people back in life. And it's one of your inner critic's favourite warnings that it uses to protect you from shame or embarrassment: "What will they think of you?"

Next time you hear "What will they think of you?" or "What will they say about you?" inside your head, here's what you do:

- » Stop and pay attention.
- » What is it your inner critic is afraid "they" will think? Ask it.
- » What is it afraid will happen if they think this? Ask it.

Then, remind your inner critic that people often don't care because they're too busy worrying about their own lives and what people think of them! These three steps will free you up and give you more choice about what to do next rather than play small at life because you're reacting to what your inner critic says.

CALL TO ACTION

Now the most fun part of all. If it really didn't matter what people thought of you, like if you *really didn't care*, what would you do? How would you act? What would you wear? Where would you go? What would you say? Who would you say it to? Go on, cut loose!

_____
_____
_____
_____
_____

We live in a world that wants you to fit in a box and not dream big. It is that sentiment that has us walking around like robots, half alive.

Let your life be a battle cry against the part of you, which is in all of us, that says your dream will never come true, that you shouldn't risk it. That part of you that tames your wild and brilliant potential by whispering, "What will they think?"

To hell with what they think!

This isn't the waiting room. This is your life. Live it with all you've got, with every ounce of your heart and soul.

Every once in a while look at yourself as you pass the mirror and say, **"You are one hot thing. I love how you are being you today."**

And if you can't bring yourself to be that nice to yourself then at least say, **"You are enough and you're safe with me."**

ROMY AND BEAR TALK ABOUT GROWN-UPS AND LOVE

BEAR: Why do grown-ups stop loving themselves?

ROMY: Because they forget who they are, Bear.

BEAR: That's sad, Romy. Because then they are sad when they don't need to be.

ROMY: Exactly. But it's not their fault. They just get lost and then other people who want them to feel they are not enough tell them that if they buy this thing or that thing they will feel better.

BEAR: Does it work? Do they feel better because they buy that thing?

ROMY: For a minute, but then they get sad and feel empty again. And so they keep looking for that full-up-enough feeling everywhere except where it is!

BEAR: So how do they find that full-up-enough feeling again?

ROMY: They remember that they are a piece of the magic meteorite dust and were once a cute little baby like you, Bear.

BEAR: You're cute too, big brother.

ROMY: But I am not a baby anymore. I will be six soon.

BEAR: You're crazy, Romy! We are always a baby inside, deep down in the place grown-ups are trying to fill.

LOVE IS A ROLLER COASTER

GIVING LOVE

"I love you" is so easy to say and so bloody hard to do. Don't believe anyone who tells you'll fall in love and never argue or lose the plot with each other, that when you find the right person that's it – smooth sailing. Real life isn't always happy ever after. Love will test you like nothing else. It will bring up all the things you need to face, all the dragons you need to slay so that you can get bigger on the inside. Sometimes you might not like the person you fell in love with. And sometimes you might hate them. That's part of the roller coaster. Falling in love is just the ticket you buy to get on.

Some people can't accept love, because they don't think they're worthy. These people might throw your love back in your face. That's OK. It's not you. Your love is not the problem. They just aren't ready yet to accept the love you have to give.

But if you are with someone who makes you feel small and chips away at who you are, someone who doesn't encourage you to be yourself because that threatens them, then that's a different story. The most loving thing you could do then for yourself and them is buy a ticket for a different roller coaster.

I SEE YOU

Standing at the bus stop thinking everyone is looking at you

Wanting to swim in the sea but afraid of how you will look

With your mum in the car, wishing she would stop talking and asking you how you are

With your mum in the car wishing she would talk to you and ask you how you are

And how you can't wait to get out of this town

In class wondering why you are wasting your life with this shit when you are not going to need it where you're going

Wishing you hadn't been so mean and said those things

Comfortable in your own skin in the crowd, saying nothing, enjoying just being there

Crying in your room

Screaming into that pillow against your face, screaming away the pain

I see you cutting to punish yourself so the pain can take away the feelings

Eating to forget

Vomiting to feel better

Stealing money out of that purse and feeling ashamed because your ma is sound

Longing to be touched

Jealous as fuck

Drinking to escape

Snorting to fly away

Smashing it all up to get rid of the feelings

Wishing they would understand

Scared to open your mouth in case they all laugh

Wanting to be anywhere but here

Walking your dog, thinking about everything

Wanting to be hugged

Caring about your family so much it hurts

Missing them so much it feels like you will die

Wondering why they left

Feeling a hundred different things in the same moment

Bikes lying all around you in the park as you laugh your heads off with your mates hoping this day lasts forever

Loving your granny because you never feel judged when you're with her

Lying so you can see your friends and don't need to explain yourself

Hoping someone would just say something and break this awkward silence

Praying to feel anything else but this

Listening to your parents arguing and wishing they would stop and just for once be nice to each other

Going to sleep with nothing to eat and feeling more shame than hunger

The next day in school fighting to pay attention because you don't want to be like your father

I see you smiling, that beautiful, one-in-seven-billion smile

Perfect

Chapter 8
MAKE IT BETTER

THE WORLD NEEDS YOU

Our world needs people like you. The adults have failed the test. They've been shown not to be up to the task of ensuring the survival of our species. They could not step up to the plate. They were too selfish and unable or unwilling to face their fears. So when they call you the cotton-wool generation and tell you to get your head out of your phone and say that once you've finished school and have a degree like them then you can have your say about the important things, remind them that you are the generation that has lived through:

- » A great recession
- » A war on terror
- » A pandemic
- » The realisation that our planet may not survive
- » Some of the weakest leaders in the history of the world

SO WHO ARE THEY TO TELL YOU TO WAIT TILL YOU'RE OLDER TO HAVE YOUR SAY?

CALL TO ACTION

The funny thing about power is if you make enough noise, "they" will have to listen. So make some noise. Make them listen to what you want to make better.

If you had the power, what would you change?

_____
_____
_____
_____

WE'RE IN THIS TOGETHER

I'm angry today. I want to break something. I know how to express my anger so it doesn't consume me, but I don't want to play nice right now. I want to taste the full sour taste of my rage. I listened to my friend Sib – one of the most beautiful souls I have ever known – talk about the times he felt alone and stared-at because he was the only black kid in a room of white people. I felt something stab me in the heart. It was regret. I was one of those shades of white in that room and I was never brave enough to ask the question I wanted to ask in case someone said, "You can't ask that." I wanted to ask Sib what it's like to be the only Black person at the party. Maybe then he would have felt less alone. But I didn't, in case I got it wrong. I wish we could strip away the constraints of "should" and "shouldn't" and have the curiosity to ask the questions we would have asked as children.

ROMY AND BEAR TALK ABOUT WHAT MATTERS MOST

BEAR: Romy, you seem sad.

ROMY: Yes. I'm sad for my friend.

BEAR: Why are you sad for your friend, Romy?

ROMY: I saw a grown-up with the same colour skin as my friend on the news last night and some people were very mean to him because his skin was black and I am worried my friend was watching it and might be scared of people with white skin like me.

BEAR: Why does it matter what colour your skin is? Like, your eyes are blue, Romy, and my eyes are brown and that doesn't matter. I don't understand.

ROMY: When people are like you and me, Bear, they are very intelligent. They know that we are all the same. We are all a piece of the magic meteorite dust, and it's just that meteorite dust comes in different colours on the outside, but it's still the same magic on the inside. But grown-ups can be very stupid. The bigger their fears get, the more they need to feel better than other people so they don't feel so scared. So they create stupid ideas like one colour of skin is better than another.

BEAR: Do grown-ups ever grow out of their stupid ideas?

ROMY: Some do. Some realise that they've only learned these ideas from another stupider grown-up and they try very hard to unlearn everything that stops them from seeing the truth. Some don't, Bear, and their hearts just get heavier and heavier until they see a rainbow and they think it's ugly.

BEAR: What? Wow! They must be no fun at playtime. And what about the ones who learn to forget everything they learned from the even stupider grown-ups? What do they remember is the truth?

ROMY: That we are all in this together and everyone needs each other. Even the aliens with fifty-seven eyes need each other. And it makes no difference how you look. The thing that matters is how much love you send out from your heart.

JUDGEMENT

We all judge. It begins early in our lives as our brain's way to categorise the world so we can navigate it. It makes our world safe. That person is from my family. That person is not. That person looks like me. That person doesn't. And on it goes. We become very good at judging who and what is around us so that we can understand and manage our environment. But like with a lot of what makes us human, when it goes from being a conscious process (you know you are judging or categorising) to an unconscious one (you are unaware when you're making judgements), it goes from being a gift to a curse. It becomes a curse when we judge without questioning our judgements and when we use our judgements of others as a method to ease our pain and soothe our feelings of vulnerability.

If you are the one who receives the hard edge of people's pain when they are hating on you, just remember:

HURT PEOPLE HURT PEOPLE.

These people are in such pain that the only way they can feel better is to try to transfer their pain to you. And they are so afraid of the world that this is their way of protecting themselves. It doesn't make it OK or excuse their behaviour, but sometimes understanding where something is coming from makes it easier for you to realise that IT IS NOT ABOUT YOU!

If you are the one who makes people feel your pain when you are hurting, I am sorry you are in such pain. I am sorry you are so afraid and scared. I hope one day you realise that it will only get worse and your wounds will never heal while you are scraping at them by hurting others. Be nicer to yourself to start with, and then you won't need to hurt others to make yourself feel better. I guarantee that if you are nicer to other people, you will start to feel better, your wounds will begin to heal and you will feel stronger. It is the wisest thing you can do because you are the one who starts to feel better.

Be the type of person who notices someone's magic meteorite dust when they don't and show it to them. Look for something special in others and then tell them about it. That's as powerful as thunder, lightning and a tornado all at once. Except rather than cause damage, it positively changes the world.

Positive words (left side):
The Best
Special
Loving
Cute
KIND
Creative
FUNNY
Cool
BRAVE
Courageous
HANDSOME
Bright
CHARMING
Friendly
SMART
Generous
UNIQUE
Beautiful inside and out
LOVED
Fun

Negative words (right side):
GAY
SPA
Geek
Ugly
PUSSY
Nerd
Loser
Pig
FAG
Bastard
THICK
PUFF
Wimp
FREAK
Slimeball
HOMO
MUPPIT
CLOWN
Tool
FATSO
Fridget
PEST

KINDNESS

"Everyone you ever meet is finding life hard, so go easy on them and just assume they are struggling.

Be kind to them. Include yourself in this. Go easy on yourself too.

You are doing the best you can right now."

Positive words (left side): Kind, GENEROUS, Special, CHARMING, Inspirational, CREATIVE, Unique, BEAUTIFUL Inside to Out, Brave, SMART, Loving, LOVED, Cool, FUN, Great Friend, Great Person, STRONG, The Best, LIT, Amazing

Negative words (right side): Nasty, TRAMP, Loser, Ugly, NERD, Bitch, Stupid, Muppit, FRIDGET, Geek, FREAK, SLUT, WEIRDO, Fugly, LESBO, Idiot, THICK, Mongo, WEAK, Waste of Space, ANOREXIC

WE'RE THERE FOR YOU

There were a hundred girls crammed into a room so small that many of them had to sit on the floor. There was bitching and slagging going on, and sometimes it went too far. The teachers wanted it to stop as they knew some girls were finding life tough.

A question was asked: "What is it about you the group might never know?"

There was silence except for shuffling in chairs and nervous coughs in the thick air. Then one girl stood up at the back and said, "I have one." She was small. Her hair was dark brown and it covered her face like curtains she wanted to keep closed.

"What people don't know about me is that my mum is sick. She can't leave her bed. It's been that way for a year now. Because my mother can't work, my dad goes to work earlier to pick up extra shifts, and so when I get up in the morning my job is to get my younger sisters ready – dress them, make their breakfast, make their lunches and make sure they're ready for school. We go in to kiss my mother goodbye and then I have to get them to school and then get myself to school. In the evening I do the same routine for dinner, and when I've put my sisters to bed, I try and get some homework done."

There was silence, but now it was a different silence, one of respect.

One of the girls on the other side of the room spoke up: "What do you miss most from before your mum was sick?"

The girl looked down, and when she looked back up, she had pushed her hair back and tears were streaming down her face.

"Before my mother got so sick that she couldn't walk anymore, she used to get my uniform and put it on the radiator so that on the cold mornings when I put it on it would feel nice and warm against my skin. It was like our little thing. I knew she was showing me how much she loved me by doing that. That's what I miss most of all. I'm sixteen and it feels like I have to be responsible for everyone and all I want is to be a little girl and have my mum take care of me."

There was no longer silence when the girl stopped talking; the sound of crying spread through the room. One girl stood up and said she had never known any of this and that she was sorry for the times she had made fun of the girl. Others stood up and apologised for how they had treated her.

She just nodded and said, "It's OK."

As the girl was sitting down, another girl shouted, "You are so fucking brave and we'll all make sure we're there for you." Then applause broke out that was loud enough to be heard throughout the school.

We never know what someone is going through. We can't, because people don't talk about how hard life is for them sometimes. So be kind. Treat people with care even when you are in pain, because you just don't know what others are going through, and you don't know when you'll need someone to be kind and decent to you.

Sometimes when we are at our lowest, the way out of that dark place is to shift our sadness by helping others. This can be in the smallest of ways. Anything that lets others know that you see them can change their world. So don't be fooled by what people want you to see so you don't see their pain. Look deeper, especially past the acts of those who seem to deserve it the least but need it the most. And just be kind to them, with a smile or a word. I know that's hard sometimes. Sometimes I don't care about anyone but myself. That's OK too. But don't let it stop you pulling others up from the depths of their lonely despair. Because when even one of us is better, we're all better off.

Chapter 9
YOUR PARENTS ARE IDIOTS AND SO ARE YOU

YOUR PARENTS ARE IDIOTS

OK, your parents might be lovely people who mean well and try their best. Most parents are nice people, and every parent is trying their best, even if it doesn't look like this from the outside.

But this is why your parents are idiots: they are very possibly unaware of who they are, why they are here and where they are going. They are asleep at the wheel. You see, they grew up in a time when emotions were not something you sought to understand or transform. Some feelings were allowed and some were not encouraged. That was just the way it was. So your parents are trying to help you find out who you are when they have never had the opportunity to find that out for themselves. They don't have the map to guide you.

I really feel for your parents, though. They're doing a job for which they received no training. They carry a lot of responsibility. Many have to work jobs they hate and feel trapped in their circumstances and can't see a way out. Some have forgotten who they are to the point that every day is a pain fest they have to endure and get to the end of without hurting themselves or you. Some of them would love to be closer to you but don't know how. Others are in relationships where they feel unfulfilled, unloved, unseen, unhappy or lost. When you look at your parents as frightened grown-up children doing the best they can, perhaps you too can feel a certain love for them that comes from realising that they are in fact doing their best. They cry themselves to sleep as well, you know, or they would if they knew how to. They long to feel whole, to be themselves as well. They miss their friends who have passed on or who they don't see any longer. They would love for their mum or dad to hold them just one more time and tell them everything will be OK. They are just like you.

So while your parents are idiots because they've forgotten who they are and might be lost, we are all idiots. You're an idiot, and I'm an idiot. And that's OK. We're all asleep or at various stages of waking up. That's why we're here – to wake up and remember who we really are. But here's the thing – you can be the one to wake them. As you discover who you are, through you, they'll see what happens when you fully step onto the stage that was always waiting for you, and whether it's with a roar or a silent whisper that you go about being you, they'll watch, and you'll give them the permission they've been waiting for.

So do your wonderful, lost parents the greatest act of love and be who you want to be. One day they will come to you and thank you for freeing them from the chains that have kept them feeling smaller than they know they were born to be. Like you, they are wiser than they realise, and they just need you to help them remember.

For those of you who don't have parents to be there for you and feel let down by every adult out there, I want to say to you that I am sorry you have felt so alone. I'm sorry that you have had to fight for every step you've taken. I wish it had been different for you. I'm sorry that no one was there for you to help you find your way, to explain why bad things happen, to wipe your tears and your knees, to remind you that you are a piece of the magic meteorite dust and that you fucking matter. I'm sorry there was no one there at the end of a day when you needed someone to talk to, to just listen. I'm sorry there was no one there in the middle of the night when you woke up terrified of the monsters in your imagination. I'm sorry some of those monsters were not just in your head.

I hope you take all the pain you have felt and you use it to fire you in the direction you want to go. And I hope that one day, when you have children of your own and you kiss them goodnight and as you ask them their favourite thing about their day and they say it was you, you'll know it was all worth it. So stay with it, Lionheart. You are not really alone.

Chapter 10
DEATH

ROMY AND BEAR TALK ABOUT WHAT HAPPENS WHEN WE DIE

ROMY: Bear, can I ask you something?

BEAR: Of course, Romy.

ROMY: I'm trying to remember where I came from, but it's been five years since I landed on earth. But it feels like thousands of years because the grown-ups have filled my head with so many things, like "be nice", "eat your dinner", "watch out not to fall", and so many other things that my head has cluttered my heart so much that my soul seems to have gone quiet forever. Please, can you help me remember where I came from and why I'm here.

BEAR: Ah, Romy, of course. I might not know as much as you do about the world but I remember everything about where we came from and why we're here. You came from the place every person on the face of the earth – all seven billion of us – came from, and that is our real Home. In this home we don't have bodies to weigh our souls down. We are full of light and we shine like a hundred million billion stars. And when you were in this place you made a decision to come here so you could forget about who you really are, only to remember again, remember that you are a soul – a piece of magic meteorite dust.

ROMY: Why would I forget only to remember, Bear?

BEAR: Because it's like when you lose something you love and you think it's gone. You're sad but then you find it and you love it so much more than you did before.

ROMY: That makes me feel warm in my heart. Oh, Bear, thank you. I thought I had forgotten forever.

BEAR: Is it clear now, my lovely brother?

ROMY: As clear as your beautiful lovely brown eyes, Bear. But now I know where I came from and why I'm here. But do I go back to the same place when I die and does everyone go there?

BEAR: Yes, Romy, all people go there. And everyone has a time that they agree to go back. No matter what they did here, no matter how bad they feel about themselves, they still go Home. Even if they did not remember who they really are or why they are here, they will still go Home.

ROMY: If we all go to that place where we shine like a hundred million billion stars, why do I hear grown-ups talk about how afraid they are of dying?

They seem so afraid of dying that this fear stalks them like a shadow and some don't even know it's this fear that is running their lives.

BEAR: Well you see Romy, what happens is they develop their personality – that's like their name and all the other things on the outside. It's like the outside of their toy box. And they begin to think they're the box and not the toys inside. They're so afraid that something will happen to the box and their worst nightmare is that it breaks. And so grown-ups spend their lives trying to keep busy so they never have to stop and think about the truth that one day the box will break, no matter how hard they try to pretend it won't. And because they've forgotten about the toys inside, they think that when the box breaks it's all over forever.

ROMY: But it's just not true, Bear. It only gets better because when they die, the box is forgotten about and it's just toys, toys, toys. Are you afraid of dying, Bear?

BEAR: Of course not, because I know where I'm going to. And because I know what happens when I get there. Do you want to know what happens when we go back Home, Romy?

ROMY: Please. Please, Bear, I'd love to know so I can remember.

BEAR: It is like the biggest party you can ever imagine. Everyone you ever loved and everyone that ever loved you will be waiting for you. Granda, Granny, Nanna, Gagga and even Momma and Dadda, and any of your friends that went Home before you did. They will all be there to hug and kiss and sing and cheer for you. They send all the love they ever felt for you straight through to your heart and the feelings are better than having hot chocolate with marshmallows every day of your life.

ROMY: Wow, Bear! I am so lucky to have a wise baby brother like you who knows all about what happens when we go Home.

BEAR: And we have each other, Romy, to dry each other's tears and laugh whenever we feel like we're forgetting. And we will always help each other remember where we really came from and who we really are.

ROMY: Yes, Bear. We are the toys, not the box. And we won't ever let the grown-ups whose eyes have stopped shining tell us their crazy ideas that we are here for any other reason than to love.

BEAR: That's it, Romy, we are here to love.

ACKNOWLEDGEMENTS

Thanks to Amy Bermingham and Jack Goodman for agreeing to read *The Teenager's Book of Life* and ensure it was honest and real. You are stunning humans!

Thank you to Siobhán Earley for pushing me in the direction I dreamed of going and reminding me to remember who I really am.

A special thank you to Hal and Sidra Stone who took me in at a pivotal stage and helped me so much. Thank you, Tamar Stone, for your continued guidance through new territory. And to the New World Library for giving me the permission to feature a passage from Hal and Sidra's book *Embracing Ourselves*, which I highly recommend.

Thank you to Philippa Keogh for her unwavering support.

To Jerome for listening to me read from *The Teenager's Book of Life* as your bedtime story.

A special thanks to T. J. Flynn for always being a trusted writing sounding board and great friend.

To Chenile Keogh for her openness and care for the production of this book and Robert Doran for his precision, professionalism and gentle touch as he led me through my first time editing a book.

To Keira, Jerome and Jesse for being the inspiration behind much of the content in this book.

My thanks to a great friend and special soul Sibusiso Buthelezi for allowing me to include his image – you are the coolest man I know Sib and thank you for teaching me an invaluable lesson.

Thank you to Andrew Brown for his imaginative cover creation and his patience in the iterative process.

To Hazel Breen, who provided the design and illustrations and so much more for this book. Thanks for your constant encouragement and support of me, Hazel. It was a joy to work with you on this.

Thank you to Stephen Rogers and Emily Lyons for their kind help in sourcing photographs.

To all the many teachers I have had the blessing of learning from throughout my life.

I would also like to acknowledge two people who are no longer with us but whose photos were pinned to the table at which this book was written. I felt their presence throughout the process. They are my grandmother, Bella Collins, and Colin Barry, a heroic young man who inspired us all.